OVERCAST

BY
MERLYN E. SEITZ

Bloomington, IN  Milton Keynes, UK

AuthorHouse™
1663 Liberty Drive, Suite 200
Bloomington, IN 47403
www.authorhouse.com
Phone: 1-800-839-8640

AuthorHouse™ UK Ltd.
500 Avebury Boulevard
Central Milton Keynes, MK9 2BE
www.authorhouse.co.uk
Phone: 08001974150

This book is a work of fiction. People, places, events, and situations are the product of the author's imagination. Any resemblance to actual persons, living or dead, or historical events, is purely coincidental.

© *2006 Merlyn E. Seitz. All rights reserved.*

No part of this book may be reproduced, stored in a retrieval system, or transmitted by any means without the written permission of the author.

First published by AuthorHouse 4/8/2006

ISBN: 1-4259-1074-2 (sc)

Library of Congress Control Number: 2005911382

Printed in the United States of America
Bloomington, Indiana

This book is printed on acid-free paper.

Author's Note

Michigan has always been a mysterious mixture of the natural wonders of lake, rough and primitive landscapes, and the often-harsh concentrations of man-made industry. However, the vacationing and playful populace from surrounding areas has seldom frequented the portion of the state in the southeast.

The following story is set in this part of the Great Lakes State, the place where I grew up. I will always be grateful for the people and places of Monroe County and especially London and Exeter townships. The flat contours, seemingly ideal for agriculture, were stolen from the swampy soil of the eastern end of Lake Erie. It demanded courage and perseverance from those who settled there. Those who settled there are the people who formed the society that gave me life and an imagination. The darkness of the skies and darkness of the sandy soil shaped my view of life and the way to live it.

The story that is told in the following pages came from my imagination. Any similarities to others who have lived there or to myself are completely coincidental and equally a part of my imagination. The story of Reed Shilllinger and the other characters never happened in real history. However, there is a reality to the journey of Reed and his companions that does not need to be chronicled in documentable history.

I am forever grateful to Carolyn, my wife, for choosing me as her life's companion, to my brother Mike and sister Juanita for sharing the growing space of London and Exeter Townships with me, and to my parents, Emory and Belva for rooting me there.

Chapter One

The small boy walked resolutely down the rutted lane between the two rows of barbed wire fence. The sky overhead, divided into layers of gray and black, rolled, changed, and butted against itself as it flew from left to right. Two hundred yards ahead of him the dark stand of leafless trees split. His destination was the gap. The boy was five years old, thin, with straight blond hair that fluttered outside the band of his cap. Under the faded denim overalls with tiny brass fasteners, the boy wore a flannel shirt with one pocket torn away, and over everything he wore a nondescript coat unbuttoned and flapping in the strong autumn breeze. The boy was Reed Shillinger.

The dry grass moved and rustled under the barbed wire on each side of the lane. At regular intervals, posts that held the wire tipped forward, backward, to the side, seldom perpendicular to the earth. The path of the boy's walk swerved to the right and left as if to avoid being snatched by the posts as he passed. There was a purpose to Reed's walk; to discover, to play, to spend some time, until someone called him to evening chores in the barn behind him.

From far away in time and space other sounds occasionally intruded, pulling him from the lane. The pull was from a place darker and warmer. He felt strange energies within that gave him a sense of largeness, a force pumping him to a giant's size. In those moments he would stop walking, lose sight of the woods and lane. The pressure of the darkness and the growing largeness within blinded him to the place around him. Then, regaining his space, the ruts, the lane, and the wind returned, and he walked again.

As he came near the gap between the woods, the wind moaned, seducing and cajoling the boy to enter. There were no words; no sound other than the groans of a creature barely alive, experiencing life for the first time, or tenuously struggling to hold it. The boy stopped, his blue-gray eyes squinting. He stared into the leafless underbrush of the woods. Another living thing had been there and left only seconds earlier. Reed's body stiffened, stepped back abruptly. He was unafraid. In a matter of seconds he made friends with the shadows, the wind, and the unarticulated sounds of the woods.

He squatted and duck walked through the opening in the thorny, stiff sticks of brush. His head was bent as he entered the woody dimness. He saw movement. This time the fear overwhelmed him. He fell flat on his stomach, and from the deep leafy carpet he looked up to see a man walking, almost running, a few feet from him. Reed held his breath. The full length of the man was invisible because of the veil of undergrowth. Reed could see a piece of rope drag protesting along the ground at the man's feet. His eyes followed the rope upward. At first it appeared to be tagging along like a mutant pet. But as Reed saw more of the man, he noticed the man's hands hanging empty at his side.

Around the man's neck the rope ended with a huge knot and circle.

A lurching commenced inside of him, and Reed felt precariously out of control. A chaotic thrashing began in the brush. Darkness and the afternoon overcast alternated in momentary modulations like heat lightning across a summer horizon. Then it completely engulfed him. The trees, the autumn dampness, the wind, and the animal motion of the trailing rope faded away. A warm uncomfortable wetness spread over Reed's body. Anxiously, Reed pulled at his clothes and rolled from side to side. He looked up and saw nothing. His eyes were open, but everything was black. He was alone. Reed rubbed his forehead and discovered that he was covered with moisture. Somehow he had fallen into the tank next to him.

The tank next to him! He stretched out his left arm, and touched the cold, metal firmness of the tank. His sense of hearing also returned. He listened for the steady watery sound of the tank. It was there! He was there! Normal breathing returned. As he looked around he realized that a powerful force had pulled him from the floor of the woods and inflated him from a five-year old body to the giant body now seen along the line of his nose. A force had transported him out of the gloom-gray overcast of the woods into the blackness surrounding the bed next to the rainwater tank on the second floor of the Day Road house. That tyrannical but beneficent force had mercifully yanked him through time to the safety of the present.

Chapter Two

Reed sat on the edge of the sleeping cot. "Shit!" he exploded. The half-whispered expletive revealed the sadness and frustration of his state of mind. Since returning to Day Road, five months ago, what was supposed to be a spiritual and renewing journey back to his roots had suddenly become a long and punishing ordeal. His life had become a series of ominous, de ja vu-like thoughts, memories from unknown recesses of Reed's mind, and dreams like the one from which he had just awakened. He sat there with his head in his hands. Slowly, he began to weep, feeling an overwhelming grief for himself. It was as if the small Reed in the dream woods was wrapped in the huge Reed's body. The weeping was that of a helpless, afraid, and angry little boy. The weeping ended when Reed asked the darkness for help; when the repetition of "What is happening to me? What should I do? Damn it! I cannot handle much more of this," ended. Reed wiped his eyes, tore the sheet from the cot, and dried his sweat-drenched body. He could see a piece of the sky through the small east window of the upstairs room. "It must be close to morning," he said and threw the sheet on the cot.

This Reed was no longer slender. He was tall; over six feet. His hair was still wispy but no longer had the lightness of a child's hair. The hair had a dry brown look after enduring years of absentminded care and grooming. It did not appear to belong to Reed. In front it wrapped over the forehead, the right side wiry and defiant, and the left side crushed and whirling in four directions. The whole effect when seen by others was a pleasant one but, Reed's self-description was that he looked like a person assembled from the main frames of two other persons. From the waist up he looked like a flat-stomached sumo wrestler. His torso was the shape of the first inch of the top of a bud vase. Attached to that torso was a set of arms, longer than average, with large thick wrists at the ends of them connecting hands that were stubby and wide. His lower half, slender and athletic, supported his thick and muscular torso. Reed's body was like a puzzle. His calves were almost as long as his thighs, and he walked with a cautious saunter. He never ran anywhere. He never looked at the ground in front of him. His walk and pace were seldom interrupted by turns, obstacles, or thoughts about where to go next.

Reed's days were full of blank spaces where plans should have been. Yet, there was no need to stop moving simply because he had no plan for the next moment of his life. Like other days, this one began with the grayness of dawn, the sweat of anxious sleep, and the terror from within. He walked to the door of the room, stepped to the landing, and carefully made his way down the wooden steps. The house complained. Each step protested his weight, his presence, jealous of his freedom to escape the dark earth beneath and the gray sky above. He had returned after years of walking in the light. The protest of each step and the cry of something sane inside would not go away.

Chapter Three

Reed stayed! He stayed when it seemed that there was nothing in his future. His life was empty of all tomorrows. There remained yesterdays, dark subconscious yesterdays were all that remained. With his last visit to Sam and Daisy's he came to stay. In a closet in Texas were several Kuppenheimers and a few pairs of Florsheim wing-tips. Everything in that Texas closet belonged to Reed's phony life; his surface life. He stood on the doorstep of the Shillinger house in Michigan dressed in jeans, a tacky pair of Reeboks, and an University of Michigan sweatshirt whose rubberized letters were cracked and indistinct. The imprint said something like "Me Again?" until Reed raised his arms and the "Me" became "Mi", the "ch" reappeared from nowhere, and the complete name of the Wolverine state magically unfolded across the front.

It had been twenty years since the last time. There was no fanfare or welcome home feast. He came alone. The simple fact that he was alone announced to Sam and Daisy that Reed had failed. Without the wife and the children, they knew that Reed had not changed. He was still the relationship bumbler that he had always been. They managed to greet him warmly and politely. There was the quick and obligatory kiss between mother and son; the handshake and indirect meeting of glances between son and father.

"Is something the matter, son?" said Daisy, "Are you sick? Where are Evelyn and the kids?"

"They didn't come - they won't come, Mom! I'm here alone. To stay!"

"Well, we're glad to have you!" Sam slammed into the dialogue, "We sure are! How long can you stay?"

"I'm here to stay, Dad! Can I have a few days until I get work and settle in?" Reed hurried on, "I'm going to find a place to live. Here. For a while."

That was six months ago. Reed did find a place to stay. He chose to return to the fear - that dark genetic fear inside – put there when he was a boy. The place was the old house on Day Road. The work was caretaker of the dormant farm land connected with the house and barns. Reed's decision to take the job, $100 a week, and a room came on his first trip to Maybee, the little town just two miles from the place.

Maybee! What a strange village! It was the kind of place that's left over at the end of dreams. The neglected asphalt road that leads into the town from the northeast caromed off the DT & I tracks that pushed their way discourteously into the center of the old village. The mill sat alongside the tracks on the southwest side of the village just before the railroad tracks fled south to Toledo. The mill was there to serve the needs of farmers scattered over the black, sandy, and prehistorically swampy soil of London and Exeter townships. The people of Maybee were there because this town was their destiny. Eventually, the road that bumped and swerved along the tracks took the traveler past a few brown and aluminum sided houses on the edge of town. These were occupied by families of tired auto workers; sons and daughters of old men and women who more often than not still lived in worn out farmhouses next to sagging barns. They waited there for the end of their boredom and the end of their wasted efforts in years of digging and jabbing the soil into reluctant harvests.

As Reed drove Sam's '62 tan Chevy pick-up into the village, he struggled to reestablish a sense of belonging. The tall rotting light poles of the village baseball field stood in the distance. As a teenager, Reed played there with his friends; but the unpleasant memory of his mediocre athleticism crushed his recollection and yanked his gaze from the field to other scenes along the road. "There's old Bill's house. The barber!" He said to himself. He had successfully changed the subject of his thoughts. The white house, modern two decades ago, had a second story that hung over the front of the rest of the house giving it the appearance of being wider up than down. Several dated models of cars sat helter-skelter along the lane leading to the house. There were several men standing under the overhang near the sparse stoop of the front entrance. From the highway one could see the occasional puff of white smoke from their cigarettes. They stared into the distance trying desperately not to talk about life and death. The past was dangerous enough for conversation that day.

As Reed approached the crossing on the edge of the business district, he was stopped by a long line of cars with the unmistakable blue and white flags of a funeral procession. Leading the parade was the only new vehicle in town. Reed recognized Hank, the undertaker and son of an undertaker, Maybee's leading citizen. Hank never looked to the right or to the left. He could find the way to St. Joseph's Cemetery the same way a person finds his fork beside his plate. He led the mourners from his stately house in the center of town to Maybee's most populated subdivision.

The procession passed, and the main street of the village was empty. Reed drove down the street until he came to the only gas pump in town. It stood on the sidewalk in front of Coil's garage. Coil, the town mechanic and school bus driver, was sitting in his doorway. "How are ya, Coil?" Reed shouted as he got out of the truck. "Okay, Reed! Haven't seen ya for a long time. How's Sam and Daisy?"

"Doing fine. Say, who died? Just saw the funeral procession going down to St. Joseph's. Somebody I know?"

"Sure. Remember old Bill who used to cut hair down the street?"

"Of course! He was the barber for Dad and my brother for years. Was he sick?" Reed asked. He calculated that the man must have been in his eighties and slipped out of life from fatigue and old age.

"Nope." Coil answered, "Well, at least he didn't die from sickness. The word is he killed himself. He's been alone for years. Never had any kids and his wife left him years ago. Just up and disappeared one day. They say he had cancer. Doesn't matter now. Day before yesterday he blew his brains out."

An unexplainable tremor shook Reed's body as he listened to Coil's account of the barber's death. A few days earlier one of the farmers that lived west of Maybee was driving through town late at night and saw Bill standing in the lot where his barbershop had once stood. The farmer saw him hunched over a spade; working to dig a hole in the center of the lot. The farmer spread the word around that Bill was burying something. After Bill's suicide some of the neighbors exhumed the contents of the hole. Now the whole town knew that they found ancient barber tools, a pair of clippers, several combs, scissors, a bottle of lilac water, and a small carved figure of an owl. Bill's neighbors soon spoke to others about Bill's last days. Bill was found on his bed with a deer rifle lying across his body. He was wearing a pair of flannel pajamas. There was nothing left of his face. His right thumb was lazily hooked in the trigger guard of the rifle, and clutched in his left hand was a scrap of paper. Written on it in a nervous scribble were the words "The Cure."

Those around him had watched Bill sitting for hours at the kitchen table. On the last day of his life, they inquired. They visited. Bill sat next to his kitchen table staring at its surface. His hand would occasionally reach out to brush away imagined dust or crumbs.

They invited him to eat with them, but he shook his head and answered by pointing at his stove and said, "I can cook. I can take care of myself." Nothing more could be done.

Just as Coil finished with the story, they were interrupted. Henry, the undertaker, returned, pulling into the alley next to the garage. When Coil stood up, Reed went around the pick-up and prepared to leave. As he reached for the ignition, he began shaking. Stunned by the lack of control, he managed to turn the key and start the engine. The roar of the truck's engine startled him, and he hurried away from the garage. The sky was gray again. Maybee was behind him.

He was traveling along the road leading west out of the village. Soon he was passing the quiet and slightly forlorn farmhouses that a hundred years ago were new and filled with hope. Each glance to his right or left gave him another look at his past, and he was vaguely conscious of a desperate desire that this time he would find a way to explain his present. He was headed for another farmhouse that had once filled his yesterdays. His meandering probes into the subject of meaning caused him to pass carelessly over the possibility that there might be ominous and uncontrollable powers at work in his life. Somewhere between the point where he and the truck would disappear on Day Road and the village limits of Maybee, a memory, a piece of yesterday still caught in the depths of the earth of London Township began its replay. It began like a radio signal unintentionally caught and mistakenly given voice in Reed's mind. From a far away time, not of history but pre-destiny, an episode from another's story started to flash in his mental vision.

Chapter Four

Bill, the future barber, a boy of twelve sat on the bank of the Seitz Drain. The drain, actually a ditch, crossed a thin piece of farm property that began north of Bill's position near the infant village of Maybee and stretched southward until it touched the banks of the river. In all, the property was about two miles long. The Drain crossed at its midpoint. Bill was the son of William Beilert who owned the farm that was adjacent to the place where Bill sat on that day in 1904. Bill and his friends had found this place on the Drain to be the perfect setting for their playful imaginations. When the boy left his home that afternoon, he had not said where he and his friends were going. Near the end of the Seitz Drain the boys had found a large mound of grass-covered earth surrounded by thick thorny brush and undergrowth. They had talked about a plan to develop that mound into a special hiding place. On this particular day they had planned to meet in order to begin the excavation. Using the shovels and hoes which they had secretly removed from the sheds of their parent's farms, they attacked the north side of the mound where it leveled off and connected with the nearby drainage ditch. It was easy work at first. The hole gradually reached the proportions that might accommodate the boys as an entrance.

Bill was in the lead. He hacked with a hoe, pulling the soil behind so that the other boys could use the shovels to remove the dirt from the hole. All of them chattered incessantly in the way that boys do when they anticipate the accomplishing of a great feat. They planned, questioned, and argued over the best use of their new cave home when it was completed. Bill worked steadily until his hoe hit something that was hard and unmoving.

"I found something! Something's buried here!" he shouted to his partners.

"What is it? Let's see it! Is it money?" the others excitedly replied.

Bill began to dig with his fingers until he loosened the object. He turned inside the hole and exited into the huddled group of his co-workers. A silence fell over them. He held a small wood carving in his hand. It was shaped like a bird. Its face, though worn from years of moisture and abrasion by the soil packing around it, was clearly the visage of an owl. Its face was a caricature hinting by its exaggerated eyes and ears that its task was to see and hear what human beings could only surmise in farfetched and mysterious tales told in whispers around night fires and moon shadows. The likeness was carved wood in the shape of an elongated egg. It was approximately eight inches long. It rolled helplessly over and over in Bill's hands as the other boys quietly and eagerly examined it.

"It's just an old wooden bird!" one of them complained. "Ugly, too. It hardly looks like a bird."

"Maybe an Indian buried it here." said another, "My dad says that Indians used to live around here. He even saw one when he was a little boy."

Bill was not listening. He was thinking. He looked over his shoulder at the mound and at the hole. For a moment he had the urge to run from the place. But his curiosity was too persistent. Grabbing the hoe, he crawled into the hole and began hacking at the soil near the place where he unearthed the carving. While Bill paused to decide where he would dig next, the soil at the base of the freshly dug wall in front of him started to crumble, sliding slowly and unhesitatingly toward the base of the wall. Bill was mesmerized by the gradual movement of the dirt. The slide became wider and, like the retreat of a wave on the beach, began to reveal more and more of the depths of the tunnel. He thought he was seeing a face. First, there appeared a brow and a forehead; as the soil fell, he thought he saw a large dark eyeless socket and then another. Bill stiffened at the gradual uncovering of the unspeakable. He wanted to escape, but he was captive to his own need to see what no other human being had ever seen. Just when it seemed that the falling soil was fully at rest, a large chunk of it abruptly dropped away, and Bill opened his mouth screaming in horror. He was staring at the macabre grin of a skull lying quietly on its side.

Slowly the boy began to back out of the hole. Crowded around him, his friends stared at the frightened and pale face of their companion. Bill did not notice the crowd around the entrance of the hole.

"What's up, Bill? Are we done? Is somethin' the matter?" Bill heard them shout...

Bill was speechless and a volcanic sickness surged from his stomach. "Let me see!" said one of the other boys as he recklessly crawled into the fresh cave. Within seconds a scream and a dusty scramble exploded out of the cave. All of them jumped to their feet and ran. Not one word passed between them as they raced toward safe havens; and no one rested on the way. Each ran toward the north to the open field and the safety of the village beyond.

As the three boys scurried away, a shadow in the nearby underbrush moved. Another even smaller and darker child had witnessed the whole project. This child was not afraid. He felt anger rather than fear. He had come to the place because his mother had told a wonderful and tragic story to him that she repeated over and over again as he grew. Often he wandered to the place and recalled his mother's words. This was the placed where an ancient ancestor had been buried. Little Majerosky had the story burned into his mind. That ancient part of him wept and the careless poking and scraping of the three white boys caused his body to stiffen and muscles to clench. It took a bit of his will to restrain himself from attacking and hurting. At the moment he thought he could no longer hold still, the three ran away. Maj stood, brushed angry tears from his eyes and shuffled away. "Someday I will kill the anger," he said.

Bill remembered the wooden owl clutched tightly in his hand as he slouched to the ground against the smokehouse wall next to his father's barn. As if ridding himself of a lethal reptile, he pushed the owl away, into the air, and, after a long arching flight, it landed in a puff of dust on the driveway between the smokehouse and the implement shed. The boy stood to go into the house, and as he passed the spot where the owl landed, he looked around, bent over and retrieved it. As he jammed it in his pocket, he whispered, "It don't mean nothin'!" and he walked toward the house. Several months after this same person, grown to old age, blew away his aged and gray head with a deer rifle, an auctioneer was sorting through a box of junk at the dead man's house. This was the second time in his inventory that he had seen the owl and was sure that it would not bring a cent in the liquidation sale. The auctioneer put the owl in his pocket. That night after he parked his car in the garage, he dropped the owl in the drawer of his workbench.

Chapter Five

Reed's short trip to the Day Road place brought him within a half mile of the Seitz Drain. As he made the right turn westbound he was startled by a large bird which lurched into the air from a cluster of trees near the side of the road. It flew like a demon toward the truck. At the moment that its large body was about to smash into the windshield, the bird stopped in mid-air, stared at Reed through the glass, and disappeared over the top of the truck. For a moment Reed stared into the sun-blinded eyes of an owl.

Reed saw the old place on Day Road even before he made the turn. For a while he had seen it from the rear then laterally and very quickly after the turn he would see it from the front. He had come over the road that he and his sister had walked going to and from Mueller School. He was in the first grade and his sister was in kindergarten. He remembered that as he stepped into the road each day after school he reassured himself by looking across the fields toward the farm. For the first time in months, Reed Shillinger felt safe. All the frightening specters from his past retreated into a dark corner of his mind, while he savored the promised return of a primordial peace.

Reed slowed the truck to a crawl as he turned into the driveway. He stopped immediately and gave himself a test. On the left was the implement shed where once a year the slaughtered pigs were parched in kettles of boiling water to make it easy to scrape off the hair. On the right was the old farmhouse gray from lack of paint. Reed remembered that it had been white. The woodshed and the outhouse should have been straight ahead. But this was 1978. There was no need for outhouses and woodsheds. Reed pulled slowly to the gate near the side entrance to the house. The place made him feel utterly alone. The absence of sound transformed it into a place where Reed had no bearings. The ever present overcast invaded Reed and the house. Nothing moved. The yellowing lace curtains hanging in the windows were motionless though promising that indeed humans did occupy the house. An empty pair of work shoes sat on the side porch. As Reed stepped toward the porch, the door opened and a man stood in the opening. He was short and heavy set. His hair was long and curly, squeezed from under the Dekalb seeds cap that was pulled tightly over his skull.

"Ya want somethin', bud?" he said.

"Sure. I used to live here when I was a kid. I'd like to wander around for a while. My name is Shillinger. Maybe you know my family. There's a lot of them in London Township."

"Never heard of them. But Shit! Look around all you want. You can't break nothin'. You can live here if you want. I got a job at Ford's so I'm movin' out. The old fart that owns this place needs a live-in hand." the man volunteered.

Very quickly the conversation was a negotiation and exchange of information about the place, the pay, and finally the phone number of the owner. The two men took leave of each other, and Reed turned to walk toward the other buildings nearby. The man was inclined to follow at first but seeing Reed's back retreating from him, turned to enter the house. Reed was content. He wanted to be alone as he searched the home on the outside for the home that was inside. He had not walked very far when he saw a sparkle in the dusty clay of the driveway. He knew exactly what it was. He sat down like a child about to play and scratched the object out of the dirt. He held a marble in his hand. It was smooth and shiny in spite of the years it had lain there. He imagined that he heard the voices of children. He looked up and saw a childish version of himself running toward the house. The woodshed, the outhouse, and the chicken coop had all reappeared. The boy was laughing devilishly as he ran. Far behind him was his little sister, Jennie, screaming hysterically, "Wait, Reedie! Wait for me. That's not fair! You never wait for... ach" She let out a scream and fell to the ground.

When Reed saw Jennie fall, he noticed that a large shadow passed over him from behind. It was young Daisy, coming to rescue her offspring, "Reed Shillinger, if you did something to hurt your sister, I'll beat you within an inch of your life." She menacingly announced. Without slowing down she grabbed Reed by the collar of his jacket and dragged him to the place where Jennie lay screaming at the sky.

"I swallowed a big marble. Now it will be in me forever. It might poison me! Mommy, I'm dying! Help me!" Jennie pleaded.

As Reed sat there in the driveway holding the marble, he remembered the whole incident. For days afterward, Daisy listened and watched intently as Jennie sat on the porcelain metal pot. She listened for the tell-tale clink. The clink never being heard, Daisy took a stick to the contents of the pot, and with a very disgusted look on her face she searched for the marble. Reed announced to himself, "It's found." He stood up and stretched. "Why not? This house could use a real live ghost. And $100 a week will keep me in food and entertainment."

Reed was not particularly eager to meet people after his arrival. There were too many failures; too many stories begun predictive of triumph that had ended in disaster. A kind of senility had overcome Reed, not a disease from age but from the memory-smothering abundance of lost life. In Taylor, Texas there were three walking catalogs, exhaustive indexes, of Reed's inability to sustain relationships. One month after Reed left Exeter to go to college, he had his first intuition that, for him, going away was getting away. It was as if everything about home, including the memories, was left in the swirling dust of the gravel roadways of southeastern Michigan. Reed became a new person at the university. The farm, the dark skies, Sam, Daisy, Day Road., Maybee, etc. were all consigned to a world that never happened. Reed speculated that there was a serious flaw that prevented him from maintaining connections with others when they were far away. Yet, once he was married, the flaw had no relevance; so he thought. A primitive force drove Reed to believe that as long as two people were able to touch, the love would continue. Yet, somewhere in

Texas, Evelyn, son Jack, and daughter Jennifer, were living documentation that either the old Reed sickness was back or there had been a hideous and destructive metamorphosis. He left them; one day Reed packed a duffel bag, walked out the door, walked the block to the bus stop, and from there he never turned back. Evelyn and the children had become disembodied names on Reed's cast of characters. For sixteen years, Reed had lived as a "normal" man; the family part, the work part, and the costuming part had the appearance of average, building to mediocrity.

Chapter Six

As Reed drove the old pick-up toward Frenchtown along the river road, he took inventory of his assets. He had a room, one bag of clothes, and a long shelf in his brain filled with closed chapters. Immediately, his eyes were filled with hot and bitter tears. He twisted the steering wheel and braked the truck to a stop at a small park along the river. He slammed the door of the cab and walked quickly but blindly to the bank of the river. A few yards to his left there was a playground. Two small children alternately ran in circles and climbed on the swings. Their cries of delight from time to time rose above the sound of the traffic and the sound of water rushing over the dam. Reed's thoughts and emotions were locked in mortal conflict. For Reed, thoughts and emotion, rather than eliminating each other, would likely sustain the battle until both lay dead in the dry shell of Reed's body.

When he came to the edge of the river, he sat on a large boulder and looked across, the line of his sight following the dam. The river was not a great river. It flowed into the lake a few miles to the northeast. From its source, many miles away, it meandered through the lowland areas of southeast Michigan. It was seldom seen because of the dense vines and foliage that crowded its shores to the point that sometimes the river became invisible. The park where Reed sat happened to be a place where the river flattened out. There were many rocks stretching from the shore tempting a precarious crossing. The dam was crumbling in several places. The depth of water upriver never reached the top of the dam, but where the dam was crumbling, a noisy stream of water escaped to keep the riverbed covered and sparkling from one side to the other. Between the place where Reed sat and the opposite shore, at least two clumps of foliage stood in the middle of the bed, and when the water was high became bushy islands. Gradually, the sound of the children reached his consciousness. As he turned to look over his shoulder, he was startled to discover that someone had been standing within a few feet of his back. Because of the slope of the bank, his first view was of a pair of canvas shoes with a tear over the left big toe, faded jeans covering a pair of long legs, and a pair of hands, one holding a paperback book. When Reed's gaze reached the face of the woman standing there, there was a moment of recognition. The woman met his eyes with her own questioning look. Reed jumped to his feet. "Caren? Are you Caren Griffin?" he said with an incredulous smile. Any more than the simple question would have revealed the memories that flooded his mind. So he asked, "Are you Caren?"

"I was Caren Griffin," she answered, "I'm Caren Mack now. I was sitting at the picnic table when you drove up. I knew it was you when you got out of the truck, Reed. I remember that angry-sad way you walked. In fact, that was the way I last saw you twenty-five years ago."

Reed walked toward her. Instinctively but nervously he held out his hand. He knew he would eventually meet someone who had loved him. For him the decision to shake her hand was the only way to cover a growing need deep inside of him. "Caren. You've not changed a bit. You look a little older, but you have not changed. You always managed to see more than another person ever wanted to show you." The handshake was a long moment of touching her and letting go. "Are those two your children?" They both turned to the playground to look at them. She nodded and Reed searched for another subject.

There was no need to search. Caren was ready. "Reed, it's good to see you. You can believe me on that. But I heard that you lived in Texas. What are you doing here? A vacation? Is your family with you? I saw your mom in the store last week, and she told me about you. She always does that. She's so proud." Caren never let the sound of her voice die. Both knew that there was another subject, but the moment wasn't right. She talked about her children; their names, ages, grades in school, when they went through their childhood diseases, and Reed listened with attention, not to the story but to the sound of her voice. The sound of her voice thrilled him like a Christmas carol in a candlelit church.

These two had been constant companions in their high school days. Their first date had been the junior prom. Reed was so intimidated that it took three weeks to ask Caren. Her locker was next to his. They met every morning, between several classes, and at the end of the day. They said "hello" to each other, they smiled, and there were brief flashes of attraction between them. However, Reed needed to be sure that, if he asked her, she would agree to go with him. Caren agreed; eventually to more than a few dances in the school gym. Reed remained cautious with her; but he initiated an intimacy with her that was uncharacteristic of him. Caren brought a gentle and confident nature to Reed's world. There was a great deal of experimentation between them; not the least of which was that Reed discovered that outside the Shillinger family one could find persons who easily shared feelings when they experienced them, at the high end and at the low end.

Caren unlocked the deeply human part of Reed. It lasted through graduation and into Reed and Caren's sophomore years in university. They were separated by several hundred miles so the relationship simply got lost. Reed, however, never ceased to love her, to feel grateful, to wonder, even after his marriage to Evie, if his commitment to the married life would have been greater with Caren.

Reed found out that Caren, a teacher in a local school, was a single parent, and having been so for a year and a half, was discovering the difficulty of learning to live alone after fifteen years of marriage. Philip Mack, Caren's ex-husband, had left Monroe County. On the day that she got the final papers of her divorce decree, Phil called her to say that he was leaving, he did not know where he would land, and she and the children need not expect him to call, write, or visit. When Caren tried to talk to him, he hung up. His parents occasionally got word of his location and activities, and they called Caren with the news. The last conversation with the Macks had been three months ago.

From the western horizon the blue sky was gradually replaced with a gray, blurred and bordered bank of overcast as the two people talked on the riverbank that afternoon. The children had left their play with the apparatus and had begun to walk the riverbank. It was four o'clock when the two old friends stood and brushed the grass from their jeans. They would meet again.

Reed experienced a new lightness to his being. As he leaned slightly to the right to close the door of the truck, he saw a new face in the rearview mirror. It was his face, but it had lost the tense anger and he saw a countenance that was relaxed with a hint of a smile. As he drove from the park, he turned to wave good bye to Caren. Behind her the river still sparkled and the sky was blue. As Reed turned onto the River Road, he noticed that the grayness was waiting for him over Day Road.

For the first time since he had decided to return to Michigan, Reed was beginning to believe that the move might have been a very good choice on his part. Leaving Texas was necessary; there was no longer a reason to stay there. Others could argue the fact of children and a wife, but Reed had tragically discarded any emotion that connected him with his family months ago. It was not a matter of their value being diminished by Reed; rather Reed arrived at the point where he could not see that there was any advantage for them to have him near them. He had nothing to give. He and Evie had taught the children to be self-sufficient; there was no need for a middle aged father who, according to their own assessments, was unable to maintain an intimate connection with anyone. Reed left because he had to leave. Coming to Michigan was a choice that he would have preferred not to make. Yet, as he bounced along the high crowned and rolling pavement of River Road, everything that he saw looked new and friendly.

CHAPTER SEVEN

Reed felt the energy of a person with a new enterprise. It was a gift from Caren. Everything around him reminded him of hopefulness and possibilities. He was heading back to the Day Road farm by traveling River Road to the southwest. The river was to his left, and the road hugged it like a gray cat pestering and rubbing the leg of its master. The road could have been straightened by many of the county engineers of the past, but the idea never was mentioned in any office or public hearing in memory. The river was old and accepted by the inhabitants of the county. Some laughed at its name, River Raisin. Rather than sounding like a river name, it raised images of a green wax-covered box and a grocery shelf full of food that only old people eat.

There was a reason for such a strange name. The area had been originally settled by the French who explored the wilderness of Michigan before there ever was a United States or a Canada. The French explorers named everything that they saw; probably the compulsion to do so came from their habit of assuming that when you name something, it is forever yours. When the French saw this river for the first time they were impressed by the abundance of wild grapes that covered the trees and foliage along its banks. Trees and brush were thick and lush along the river, but everything that grew shared the sun, rain, and nutrients with the ever present and incessant vines of the wild grapes. This parasite so impressed the French that they gave its name to the river. Translated the river would have been called "The Grape River," however, the translation never took place. The inhabitants who eventually became English speakers simply transliterated the French name; River Raisin was the way it was known.

Reed was unconscious of the past of the place where he was traveling. The French had left unique marks of their presence in the area. The land was originally inhabited by the Potawatami tribes of North America. Their villages were located along a well-established trade road that began at Lake Erie and stretched to the west. These people were never hostile to the invading foreigners, but mutual suspicion demanded careful planning for the worst possible scenario. So the French invented a way to parcel the land to the settlers that guaranteed enough fertile growing land to each family and provided security from the primitive tribes of the area. Each claim was marked out in a strange configuration. In the minds of the French it was necessary that each farmer have frontage on the river. Secondly, it was necessary that each farmer build his house as close as possible to the next-door neighbor for the purpose of mutual protection and self-defense, and, finally, it was necessary that each farmer have enough land including wooded area, to support each family through agriculture and trapping. The solution was obvious. All the claims were surveyed and configured in a long and thin shape that became known as the "French claim." The river frontage was about 400 yards. That being its width, it then stretched for approximately one mile straight from the river, penetrating the land that lay alongside the river. These long thin strips remained in place even to modern times. Although few farmers in that area operated on an original French claim, often two properties with adjacent boundaries, when taken together, would duplicate the original French survey and map. Such was the case for the Day Road farm where Reed was staying. The farm occupied the western tip of the original claim. His family had purchased the land in the middle 1800's. The river end of the claim had been purchased by a brother of Reed's great-grandfather. Although the farm was now owned by someone outside of Reed's family, the river end of the claim was still owned by a descendent of Reed's great uncle. The predecessors on the river end had built a tavern to accommodate weary travelers along the river. That tavern was now a designated "historical" structure and occupied, not as a tavern, but as a domicile. The original claim was now divided between three farmers and the owners of the old tavern. As Reed drove past the tavern, the connections between the land over which he was driving and the land where the Day Road farm was situated were not known to him. To the right Reed could see a densely wooded area that had been left by earlier occupants of the land to supply wood for building, heating, and hunting. As the old pick-up rocked over the paved surface, it passed between the thick bushiness of the riverbank and the tall trees of the woods on the right. Dusk had settled over the area. As Reed switched on the lights of the truck, he saw a dark shadow in the middle of the road. The shadow stood over a carcass on the pavement. As Reed braked to prevent hitting it, the creature turned and looked directly at him. At the same time it spread its wings and lurched into the air. Its huge eyes reflected the lights of the vehicle, and Reed tensed behind the wheel. He was sure that for a moment he saw anger, the uncommon evidence of an emotion, in the eyes of the owl. As it rose into the air, the bird swerved to the right and quickly disappeared into the woods.

Chapter Eight

Usually, mystical moments like the flight of the owl left Reed in a pall of depression or at the very least sent him into quiet contemplation, but that night was different. The remarkable hopefulness from the chance meeting with Caren would not be dismissed by an owl in the road. He arrived at the dark farm yard still thinking of the future, and noting that his regret about Evie, Texas, and the children did not sting as it did just six hours earlier. He turned into the driveway, his eyes following the sweep of the headlights across the breadth of the huge yard that lay between the various buildings of the farm. It was instinctive for Reed to follow the lights. There was no yard light to illuminate the area at night. The beam of light bounced nervously as the truck dropped and leaped over the deep mud holes in the driveway. The beam of light began at the large barn that had been the dairy barn when the Shillingers worked the place. It swept to the right over the horse barn and the intervening ramshackle wooden fence around the barnyard. There was a gap between the horse barn and the next building; a quick glimmer of reflected light flashed toward Reed from the tall grass that had grown under, up, and through the ancient, rusting hay cutter that the last farmer had left behind. The next building was the huge tool storage barn that stood in the foreground between the road, the pig barn and the chicken complex.

As the light streaked across the last gap between buildings, Reed saw something move. He stopped the truck in the middle of the turn. He put it in reverse and backed until the headlight beam was shining exactly on the space between the woodshed and the granary. Nothing! Someone was roaming around the buildings. When he parked the truck near the entrance to the house, he grabbed the flashlight on the seat next to him and stepped from the truck.

Reed walked toward the woodshed, and a wave of prickles rose all over his body. It was dark and something or someone unknown was near. As he turned the corner into the space between the buildings where he had seen the movement, Reed walked more hesitantly and concentrated on the lighted section in front of him. He scanned and felt relief. He saw nothing. He took a deep breath. At just that moment, he stiffened in mid stride. Although he had not seen anything, he now heard the sound of heavy, uncontrollable panting. Quickly he aimed the light in the direction from which he heard the sound. It came from around the corner most distant from him at the rear of the granary. Then the breathing stopped. Reed switched the flashlight off, and he slowly and soundlessly began to walk toward the corner of the building. The breathing commenced again. Reed was aware of two sounds; the beating of his heart and the sound of breathing, ironically not his own, since he had gulped a chest full of air and held it as he skulked toward the dark end of the building. The sound of breathing was still there when Reed reached the corner, pressed himself against the wall, and planned his next move. He decided that to frighten whomever or whatever was there was the best strategy. He was not ready to physically engage the intruder. With his finger on the flashlight switch he leaped into the open area behind the building, turned abruptly, and turned on the flashlight. Crouched against the back wall, almost in the crawl space beneath the building, was a man dressed in dark clothes, wearing a wool ski cap, eyes surrounded by the dark bush of a beard, staring at Reed. In his arms he held the limp and flopping form of a small child. The child's head was suspended like a tether ball from the body which the man held with the possessiveness of an animal protecting the victim of his last kill. Instead of dropping the body and attacking Reed, the man leaped to his feet and ran into the darkness. For a short distance, Reed followed with the light, and then began to pursue the man across the field toward the ditch about 100 yards away. The man was amazingly fast. Reed dropped the flashlight as he put all his effort into running. His eyes became accustomed to the darkness, and he knew that if he could stay within twenty or thirty yards of the man he could keep him in sight. Ahead of him he saw the man descend the short slope to cross the wooden bridge over the ditch. Suddenly Reed was violently jerked to a halt in mid stride. He felt a burning and tearing across his abdomen. In the darkness a barbed wire strand, unseen by Reed had brought him to an immediate and painful halt. The barbs dug into the flesh of his midsection, and he screamed in pain. Struggling to maintain his balance, Reed backed away from his pain and the wire strand. Quickly he inspected his wounds and thought about what to do next. He could continue his pursuit of the man with the child's body, he could go to the house and wait until morning, or he could contact the police now with the possibility that he might be caught before the trail grows cold. He decided to contact the police immediately.

Anywhere else in the world calling the police was simple. However, Reed had never connected a phone on the farm. With the stunning realization that he had been thoroughly acculturated to urban and modern life, Reed rebuked himself, walked to the pick-up. The farm across the road from the old Shillinger place was the Kreutzer place. The Kreutzer family had lived there for three generations. He made the short run on the road and turned to make the long, slow run to the house at the end of the lane. He felt thoroughly exposed. The headlights of the truck were necessary to see the driveway, but, at the same time, the beams landed directly on the windows of the Kreutzer house. As he pulled the pick-up to a stop near an iron gate, he noticed that there was a light burning in the room off the back entrance. He walked to the door, up the steps, and knocked. For a long time there was no answer. Deciding that no bedroom could be that far away, he knocked again. The door swung open. It had never been completely latched. Reed could see that the room he was about to enter was the kitchen.

Reed saw that there was nothing unusual in the kitchen. The light spilled from the doorway on the other side of the room, spread across the scarred and uneven linoleum floor, and splashed upward a few inches on the walls and each piece of furniture in the room. Standing in the middle of the room was the supper table. To the left stood an old wood burning cook stove. During the winter months the families in these old farmhouses used the stoves to heat the house and to cook their meals. At the other end of the kitchen stood an electric range, and next to the range Reed saw another door. He decided to inspect the rest of the house before opening any closed doors. His first priority was to find a phone. He felt strange looking for a phone in a house where he had yet to meet its occupants. They could be very deep sleepers; comfortably curled up in their beds with no idea that an intruder was wandering around the house. "Hello! Mr. and Mrs. Kreutzer? "He stopped to listen for an answer, "I'm your neighbor. Across the road. I need to use your phone for an emergency." Reed heard nothing. With each word of his announcement he had moved deeper into the house until he could see into the room where the light was burning. Nothing was out of place. In the far corner of the room, there was a desk. There was a lamp sitting on the desk. Reed's first thought that something might be terribly wrong came when he noticed that all the drawers in the desk were open, and the contents were scattered on the floor around the desk and on its top. Even as that thought flashed through his mind, he heard a sound. It was the sound of a whimper. He turned. He looked to the left and behind and was startled to see a young boy, twelve or thirteen years old, squatting and backed into the corner of the room. Dangling from his hand was a small caliber pistol. The boy's eyes were unblinking and staring into the center of the room. Once more he whimpered. Reed could see that the boy was so terrified that he was holding his breath until he inhaled making the whimpering sound. Reed made a testing movement toward the boy. The boy did not seem to notice Reed's presence. Reed continued toward the boy, "Are you alright?" he asked. Suddenly the boy moved. With one motion he aimed the gun at Reed and focused his eyes on him. "Stay away! I can shoot this. I'll kill you." the boy shouted between uncontrolled whimpers and sniffles. Reed froze where he stood.

"I'm not going to hurt you. Where is your family? Your dad and mom? If you will call them, I'll try to help."

"Mom? Dad?" he whispered as if he were afraid that anything louder might wake them.

"They cannot hear us now. They're asleep. Dad's in there. And mom? She's with my sisters in the back yard."

Reed could feel the overwhelming squeeze of fear around his stomach and chest.

"In the backyard? What's a mother and daughters doing in the backyard at midnight?"

Reed saw the phone on the edge of the desk. Reed picked up the phone and called the operator, told her his location, and explained that something terrible had happened to a whole family. "Please call the sheriff right now. I'll be here with the young boy. I have a feeling he is the only survivor." Nodding his head he hung up and walked over to the boy. He took a deep breath. The boy was beginning to trust him. Nevertheless, Reed approached the boy very slowly and squatted directly in front of him.

"Son, you don't have to worry anymore about someone hurting you. I called the sheriff. I'm sure he's on his way." Reed spoke these words as he held out his hand to receive the gun.

"But he killed mom and dad. He dragged my sisters outside with mom. He hurt them. I know. He wants to hurt me." He began to sob near the end of his answer to Reed.

"What's your name?" asked Reed.

"Robbie. Robbie Kreutzer." answered the boy.

"Robbie, let's go outside and wait for the sheriff to come." Reed stood as he spoke.

The boy stood with Reed. The boy let the gun fall to his side. As the two of them walked toward the kitchen the sound of a siren could be heard outside. The boy hesitated at the door and Reed went through the door ahead of him. When Reed stood on the porch he could see the lights of the patrol car bouncing toward them on the lane between the house and the road. As the boy approached him from behind, Reed felt a small hand slip into his. He also heard the sound of sobbing before he looked down to see the face of Robbie in the lights of the car as it came to a stop in front of them.

The officer was saying something through his radio microphone as he exited the vehicle, but he quickly walked to Reed and the boy and began to ask questions. At one point the boy said something and pointed to the area of the yard behind the house. The three of them walked in that direction, the officer lighting his flashlight for the first time since he arrived. The darkness was complete except for the beam of the deputy's light. The huge, barren walnut trees growing around the house were dry and still, nearly invisible. With each sweep of the light all that could be seen of the trees was the first ten feet of their huge trunks as they came out of the ground. About twenty feet behind the house was an ancient dug well. It wasn't used anymore. The protecting circular wall, built of bricks, was still there, but the opening had been covered with large wooden planks. The most auspicious sight was the way the planks were now scattered on one side of the well. Someone had been in a great hurry to open the well and had left without replacing the planks. All three of the people stopped, staring at the well in the steady beam of the officer's light. The deputy was the first to approach the well. Reed followed. The boy didn't move, though he was reluctant to let go of Reed's hand. The deputy walked around the well at first. When he stepped to the rim of it, he directed the light into the well and straight down. Reed was beside him, and both of them peered down into the narrow dark tube below. They were at first slightly dazzled by the glint of the light from the dark water. Gradually, however, a face emerged from under the surface of the water. A face, but progressively, then, the dark hair of a woman and, with a rotating of the body the stark whiteness of her back split the surface of the water and dominated the view at the bottom of the well. The officer turned abruptly, grabbed Reed's arm, and led him back to the boy. "Stay here with the boy. Tell him what he needs to know. I'll call for assistance," he said as he walked to the patrol car. Reed looked at Robbie's face and knew that there was very little that he would have to tell the boy that he did not already know.

Within an hour the deputy and his assistants had made several grim discoveries. In the well they found the bodies of the mother and one of the daughters.

The father's body was in the bedroom. All of them had died from deep cuts across their throats. At the time of the removal of the bodies from the well, Reed walked the slight incline toward the well. "Deputy! The boy says that he has two sisters. I think I know where the other one is," Reed said quietly.

"I thought you said that you hadn't searched before I arrived," answered the deputy.

"I didn't. I saw the body of the other girl across the road at my place." He went on to tell the deputy the whole story of the man behind the building. The deputy was angry with Reed. If he had known that Reed had seen the suspected killer, they might have commenced a search in the fields and woods around the Day Road farm. "Let's go! I want you to show me the exact place where you saw this man," said the deputy as the two men climbed into the patrol car.

The man held the body of the girl close to his breast. Life was all about the transitions. While most human beings thought of life as that which happens between birth and death, this man was driven by the belief that life is birth and death; that which transpires in between is only the recess. Therefore, he held the body close. He ran steadily across the fields behind the farm opposite the Kreutzers' place. He was surprised when the man found him behind the shed. That was not supposed to happen. Nevertheless, the man in black felt good. He had once again participated in the miracle of death. He stopped momentarily to inspect the face of the dead girl in his arms. For him the gore of the slash across her throat had no effect. He smiled at the corpse. He could see peace on the face of the girl. A flash of memory reminded him that she ran from him when he awoke her from sleep in the house. He tried to calm her by telling her that he was going to help her; give her a gift that no one else would be able to give her. But she screamed, slipped to the other side of the bed and almost made it out of the room. He was proud of his swiftness. It made his calling so much easier. He caught the girl by the hair before she reached the door of her room. She screamed again. He threw her to the corner, pulled head back, spoke softly in her ear, "Thank you for giving your life for me," and deftly drew the long and deadly blade across her throat. His victims never understood. They were always angry and afraid; as if he needed permission to give them the best of all gifts. He understood their fear. Change is always troublesome and, sometimes, painful, nevertheless, the man wished that he could talk to each victim after killing them. He was sure that they would be grateful to him. As he came nearer the woods, his running slowed to a jog. He suspected that soon he would need to hide the body, leave the woods, and avoid people for a few days until the excitement passed.

Everything matched the night. His clothes were black. His face was hidden under the dark bush of a beard. His hair was black and shiny like coal. He was about five feet ten inches. Because of the heavy wool coat and the ancient pair of pure wool pants, he looked stocky and muscular. Everybody called him "Madge". That was from his last name, Majerosky. Few people knew that his first name was George. It didn't matter. Madge was a loner. Occasionally he would leave his farm where he tended his vineyard, venture into Maybee, or walk the country roads on foot. He liked people. After all Madge needed people. They were the creatures to whom he was obligated to give his gift. Madge lived very near the farm where Reed Shillinger grew up and was now living. In fact Madge remembered Reed as a small boy. Several times he had walked past the Shillinger farm when the children were playing in the dusty farmyard. Madge had hoped that one day he could give them his special gift. He had gone so far as to scout their house. Madge laughed as he remembered how he had peered into every window and knocked on every door before leaving them alone. Most likely they thought he was some eccentric neighbor looking for a handout. He memorized the layout of the house. Such detail was a small part of his preparation. Before each priestly act of sacrifice, Madge prepared. His work took place in the darkness. By studying his workplace in the light, Madge made friends with the darkness. His preparation for the Shillingers was wasted. Within six months they moved to another farm several miles away.

This shadow man entered the woods still carrying the body. He had a plan in mind when and if the authorities came close in pursuit. The man with the flashlight in the nearby farm yard probably called the sheriff. There was a culvert on the other side of the woods. It was large enough to hide the small body of the girl. For a moment Madge's body trembled and tingled with the fear that a fugitive feels when his capture seems imminent. Madge broke into a hard run and then a sprint through the woods. His path through the think brush and trees zigged, zagged, and lurched as if he were dodging exploding shells. He dodged to the right and to the left avoiding trees and the impediments of wild thorns and young trees. As he broke the boundary of the woods, he lunged into the drainage ditch between the woods and the road. From a crouching position he looked quickly to the right and to the left. He had trained himself to see in the night. He saw the culvert. He stood to walk toward it, pulling the girl's body close to his. He looked like a father carrying his baby to her bed. He really didn't want to let go. He bent over the mouth of the culvert, inserted the feet first, and pushed the body into it until it was invisible to anyone standing upright in the ditch.

Madge stretched, shook himself, and walked away. As he walked, he reached around his back to adjust his tool. Even on this moonless night there was a glossy glint to the grapevine pruning knife stuck in his belt and lying against his back. The handle was about eight inches long, the blade twelve inches, and, at the end, the blade narrowed slightly and curved. The dark stain covering the blade was fresh. Madge returned to his house, and carefully washed, and dried his tool. There would be a need for it again.

Reed and the deputy walked from the spot in the woods behind the shed and found nothing. "We'll come back in the morning when there's light. I'll bet there will be some tracks. Couldn't carry a body that far without leaving tracks somewhere," said the deputy. Reed noticed how the deputy never expressed the shock and grief that was hiding inside. He thought about it and smiled to himself. He remembered the way it was. Under the gray skies of London and Exeter there was little emotion expressed. Why waste a scream of pain or a shout of anger on what you can't control? The tragedy of today's event may be of no account compared to the next tragedy. Save the grieving, reserve the anger, and, go ahead, risk the chance of appearing cold and unfeeling. There was enough fear here to fill all the lifetimes of everyone who lived under the skies along the river in London and Exeter. There were no exceptions.

Chapter Nine

It had not always been that way. The river, the woods, and the rare open spaces on the western tip of what later would be called Lake Erie were once the habitat of a people who believed that the land under their feet was the special gift of the Great Spirit. Though they knew nothing of the idea of the white man's Eden, if they had, the comparison would have been obvious to them. The little river that flowed gently through the thick forest led them to the big waters of the lake where they could easily glide to many lands in the canoes they had made out of the branches, carefully cut limbs, and the bark of the birch trees. In the dense forests, which covered everything between the Maumee in the south and the lake to the north and west end of the big waters, the game was plentiful. The Potawatami tribe also believed that the Great Spirit had given them the gift of corn. They planted it in the dark sand in the clearings that occasionally broke the monotony of endless forests. The people had found it a peaceful place after the recent wars between the peoples who lived beyond the big water and others who lived to the south of the Maumee. On the site where Reed's ancestors built the tavern, the people had established a small village. For at least two generations the people lived on that site, birthing their children and burying their dead. Slightly to the north of the village was the burial site of their people. When the French came, the people no longer lived without fear. The young men of the village trained for the real possibility that the strange white skinned invaders were prepared to kill them and destroy their village. The men learned war to insure the survival of their clan. Seven miles to the north the invaders were building their own village. Their manner of building was strange and cumbersome. They cut the forest away and shaved the trunks of the slaughtered trees. They used them to construct heavy immovable dwellings with slanted covers made of smaller slivers of the wood from the trees. The people wondered what they would do with the dwellings when they had to move. There was no way that any part of a house could be bundled and carried to the next site.

This small village of the Potawatami was unlike most of the villages of the people. The people were hunters and trappers. They moved the villages from place to place following the wildlife. However, this small clan of the people discovered that along the gentle river, near the nightfall end of the big waters, there was never a time when the game diminished. During the warm months the clan cultivated the corn seed. This they had learned from their neighbors, the Wyandots. There was never a need to leave the banks of the River. A gentle cycle of life had developed for the clan. It remained that way for a generation. The change came when the French arrived. There was an uneasy acceptance of the French which continued until another group of white people began to move into the area. They called themselves the English. Occasionally, one or two of them would appear from out of the south. They came to the leaders of the clan and spoke of the evil French; suggesting that eventually it would be necessary to drive the French away. They assured the clan's elders that they were their friends and only wanted to help them. The small clan of the people continued to live as they had always lived. Then the day came when men from the settlement known as Frenchtown entered the village with strange gear lashed to their backs. They asked permission to walk the banks of the river. They placed a tubular rod on the top of a three-legged stand. One of them placed his eye at one end as if he were looking through a tiny hole in the side of a wigwam. The other one stood several yards away holding a pole with markings of different colors equally spaced from the middle of the pole to the top. Then they walked in straight lines from the riverbank north. One of them would set up the three-legged stand then the other would walk ahead. When he stopped he held the pole until the man looking through the glass wrote something in a book that he carried in his knapsack. The people did not know that this was the first step before the French would eventually divide the land of the clan's hunting grounds. Each of the divisions would be sold to French settlers who were even then trekking across the Canadian wilderness to the fort of Detroit.

The people saw the comings and goings of the white men with suspicion and fear. The surveying was mysterious to them, but, at least, it did not lead to war and bloodshed. During the time when Sihaknak was chief a third white tribe came. They spoke the same language as the English, but they came from the south rather than the east and north. They were farmers. The French had been trappers. The people of fire, the Potawatami, had seen the wars between other tribes and clans before. This time it was a war between the white tribes, the English and the Americans. Other dark skinned tribes, the Shawnee and other clans of the Fire people, joined with the warring white tribes. But Sihaknak had convinced the people of the village not to enter the struggle.

There were some in the village who disagreed with the chief. The Fire People were clan-centered communities. The chief was more or less an honorary position. They respected the leader, but absolute obedience was not required. Sihaknak belonged to the order of the Bird, and the chief advocate for joining the English against the Americans was Pokagon of the order of the Bear. Pokagon could often be seen as a boy standing at one of the bends of the river looking toward the east. He was a sullen and often cruel boy. No one was surprised when he joined the English General Proctor upon hearing of the planned attack on Frenchtown. Later the scalping of white people became Pokagon's joy in life. However, his first experience of war with the whites was very unsatisfying. Victory eventually belonged to the English, but it was an ugly battle. The settlers fought hard. Pokagon and the other Fire People with him were stunned by the ferocity. Many white prisoners were taken as the victorious English and their allies started the trek north to Fort Malden on the Canadian shore of the Detroit River. The fact that so many of the Frenchtown settlers and their defenders were allowed to remain in the village angered Pokagon and other warriors. So that night two hundred of the Fire People slipped out of the English camp at Brownstown, went back to Frenchtown, and attacked the remaining inhabitants of the town. The conquest exhilarated Pokagon. With each swing of the war club and tomahawk, with each look of terror on one of his victim's faces, and with the splatter of blood from each slash with his knife, Pokagon fell deeper into the darkness of the world of death. The next dawn Pokagon was convinced that the spirit of wendigo, the cannibal demon, had possessed him. Never before had he felt such energy. He yearned for the power of the Great Spirit. Never had it touched him until the night of the massacre. It was mid-morning when he entered the village. The children ran from him. Pokagon saw terror and puzzlement on the faces of each person he met in the village. He looked down at his body. He was covered with the gore of death and slaughter. Like a drink of cold spring water, the sight of the blood refreshed Pokagon. He began to dance among the wigwams. A song of victory and joy came from his lips. He whirled. He jumped. He felt the power to fly like a hawk. He felt the intensity that he had seen in the eyes of the bear standing on its back feet and prepared for battle. As he ran toward the children in the village, he chanted the frightening warning words of the insane, "Kill me! You look like beavers to me. I warn you, I will eat you! Kill me before morning. I am under the power of Wendigo!" Wendigo was a spirit feared most by the Fire People. It came only occasionally, but its coming sent terror through the village. Wendigo was the demon who killed and ate the flesh of humankind. Pokagon was euphoric in his trance-like dance. Sometime in the night he turned sullen and he stopped dancing. He needed to kill.

The people of the village noticed the ominous change. As was normal, they entered the squat, round-roofed wigwams where they slept, talked of the day, and embraced each other in homage to the great spirit of ongoing life. But on this night they did not sleep. With the wendigo about, the adults of each family sat in the doorways of each dwelling in anxious watchfulness. This night was a night of terror for everyone except the children. They slept secure in the strength of their elders. The family of the small boy named Shabonee wept through the night. Nashiwaskuk, the father, did not return from the foray into Frenchtown, and Pkuknokwe noted that her small son did not enter the dwelling as the terror-filled keening of the women warned that the wendigo was in the village. Throughout the long night she softly called his name. He never came.

Like people assessing the damage from a nighttime storm, the people of the clan stuck their heads out of their dwellings to see. Lying outside the door of Nashiwaskuk's wigwam were the bodies of Pkuknokwe's husband and son. Their throats had been sliced in the manner of slaughtering dogs for one of the Fire People's medicine ceremonies. Pokagon was gone. The time of mourning began with the first sound of keening. Revenge could wait. Because the Wendigo had possessed him, Pokagon was free of blame. They would never hear of him again. The horror of Wendigo is that while the demon possessed and killed through his host, eventually he would take the host into the dark world forever.

The way of the Fire People was to bury their dead in shallow graves in the forest. Because it was winter the ground was hard and unyielding, so they waited until the spring sun warmed the soil. Then the little clan planted the corn and buried their dead. Shabonee was placed in the grave with his father. Both were wrapped in skins for the journey to the world of the dead. Provisions for three days were laid with them. To the people the place of the dead was a world of plenty. The man and his son would need provisions for the journey. The bodies were covered with earth and a small wigwam was built over them. The final act of marking the place of burial was to drive a small stake in the ground at the head of the grave. A small, carved figure was tied to the stake to announce to passersby the clan to which the dead man belonged. Nashiwaskuk belonged to the clan of the Bird. Tied to this stake was the figure of an owl.

Chapter Ten

Madge hurried through the darkness from the place where he left the body of the girl. The remaining hours of darkness would give him time to walk the three miles to his parents' place. He would walk across the fields, following the fence rows instead of the roads. The sheriff always got closer to discovering him after each event of sacrifice. Madge was not afraid. He did what he did for reasons that never allowed him to think of the consequences. This dark man did what he did because it had been given to him by his ancestors. These acts of sacrifice fed the land and paid old debts. The sky above often turned gray in a mood of despair and hopelessness. Madge knew that such grayness could not remain long before someone would die.

Others would not understand. The people who would understand had been forced to leave long before Madge was born. His father and mother remained behind as guardians of the people's spirit. Now they were dead and Madge was the last.

About one half mile south of the river on a narrow crossroad stood the small squat house of the Majerosky family. No one remembers where they came from or when they moved into London Township. They were a strange couple. When the twentieth century began the area around Monroe was made up of a great diversity of people. The predominant group was the German, then the French, the Polish, and the rest. Each group except the French was new immigrants and retained the use of their language. Very few people had ever spoken with both the man and the woman who would become Madge's parents. From the beginning the couple was very reclusive. They purchased a small parcel of land that had once been owned by the same family from whom the Shillingers had purchased their farm. Immediately, as if overnight, the neighbors were surprised to see that the couple was able to put up a small lean-to for temporary shelter. The man and women lived that way from early April through October that year while the man single handedly built a small house. The man's physique would eventually be cloned by his son, but the woman was the one noticed by the neighboring farmers. They would find any excuse possible to travel by the place in the middle of the day just to stare at the strange new woman in the township.

She was a curiosity because she was a Native American woman. She was tall and slender, and her skin was the color of polished flint. While many referred to the original tribes of the Michigan dwellers as the "red men," that was only partly true. The Fire People were primarily the color of the woman. Not red but bronze and burnt. She let her hair grow freely, tying it back with a cloth into a long tail-like bundle down her back. Few people ever came close enough to notice that her eyes were dark and small. She never spoke to anyone except her husband and then to her son after he was born. While the little family lived in the lean-to, they did their food preparation over an open fire in a large kettle that hung from a crossbar that was suspended between two upright stakes driven into the ground. Every morning the woman kindled the fire and kept it alive until after the evening meal had been prepared. Morning and evening she could be seen working around the fire. Within months after their coming, the curious noticed that the woman was no longer slender. She grew thick at the waist. Everyone knew that the new couple was about to become parents. They wondered what the issue of a Polish man and an Indian woman would look like. As the months and years went by the word was spread that the couple had come from Canada; somewhere in the province of Ontario not too far away from the city of Windsor along the Detroit River. Most of each day was spent in the building of the small house that would be called the Majerosky place from its creation onward. However, the neighbors were surprised and not a little impressed when they noticed that soon after their arrival, the man began to plant small cuttings from an unknown grape vineyard far away.

The Majeroskys carefully obeyed the laws of the township and the county; including school for their young son. The residents of the area were usually very tolerant of those who might be different or live an atypical lifestyle. Of course the family seldom entered into the social or public life of the area. The woman regularly walked into nearby Maybee or further to Monroe to make household purchases. The man was often seen working in the yards of families in the villages around the area. His ability as a vintner led to his popularity as a gardener and handyman. As Madge grew, especially in the summers, the two of them, father and son, could be seen walking the roads of London and Exeter. The family never owned a car. Madge never finished high school. It was not a case where he could not do the work. Something shaped Madge into a serious, morose, and isolated boy. When he was small, he could most often be found alone among the rows of vines on his father's small farm. At other times, as he entered his teen years, Madge wandered in the woods that were near the back of their property. Along the edge of the woods Madge explored the banks of the long ditch that crossed from one side of the property to the other. Over the years, though few ever were given the opportunity to look at it, no one ever recalled seeing a smile on Madge's face. He never shaved his beard. Even when he was a young boy, the dark growth that would later be his distinguishing mark began to appear.

Madge seldom heard his father's voice. But his mother was always ready to tell Madge the stories of the Fire People, her people. He learned that over a century ago, his mother's people had lived in this vicinity. She named several of the ancestors as she told the stories of the time when they lived near the Raisin River. Madge was intrigued by the strange names and customs. In a way, however, for this lonely and reclusive boy, hearing the tales of his ancestors and discovering the idiosyncrasies of his family's past, allowed Madge to imagine a future of his own. Daily he watched his father fighting with the black sand of the farm, jabbing, stirring, and digging it to productiveness. Madge learned the ways of the farmer and vintner. He never dreamed of escaping his heritage. But Madge was determined to become something more than his father. He dreamed of his mother's ancestors. He imagined them living in the wigwams that had once stood on the soil of the Majerosky farm. Madge spent hours in the woods searching for evidence of the long ago presence of the Fire People.

As he often did in the evening after the work was completed, Madge took a small spade from the shed and walked toward the woods. In a very methodical way, Madge had begun to excavate the banks of Seitz Drain. It was his guess that if a clan of Fire People lived near this place, then surely somewhere along this ditch he would find evidence to prove it. Madge had a sixth sense about where to dig. There was not much light left in the day so he chose a place to dig that did not require the removal of small trees and underbrush. Just a few feet from the stagnant water of the drain was a nearly perfect mound but for a slight cavity that, because of the many years of grassy growth, appeared to be no cavity at all. Madge felt a sudden surge of excitement. A strong breeze had begun to blow as clouds suddenly darkened the sky. Over the rustle of the wind through the trees, Madge was startled by the loud sound of flapping wings. Madge stood upright and stared at the sky. The sound of wings faded. He saw nothing.

He returned and continued to drag the dead grass and debris from the hole at the base of the mound. He had been at this place before. Like a dream that repeats he knew he had stood here at another time, and a strange anger and alien energy filled his body. Once Madge had cleared the grass, he was able to crawl into the hole. It was an entrance. The passage was no longer than two or three feet. The area was in complete darkness. With his spade, he jabbed at the wall opposite the hole. Almost immediately he struck a hard object. In the dark Madge dropped the spade in order to inspect the object that he had struck. He reached into the hole. The object fell into his hand. It felt like a round, light-weight ball. Madge backed out of the hole into the leftover light of the evening. All the while he held the object in his hands. He did not explore its surface. He knew what he had in his hands. His first encounter was with the mocking grin of the skull; his second encounter was not with the skull at all. Like a man who has just handled some forbidden and expensive knickknack from mother's secret treasury, Madge raised his eyes and quickly scanned the woods around him. At last his eyes settled on the barren scrub trees in front of him. Two eyes stared at him from a branch high over his head; an owl, emotionless and unmoving, met Madge's gaze. Both the eyes of the owl and the object in his hands shared a stunning emptiness. A slicing streak of heat passed through his body. It started in his midsection and spread centrifugally from there. His grip on the skull loosened, and it fell from his hand bouncing and rolling until it came to rest near the edge of the ditch. Madge could see the reflection of the grotesque grin in the black water of the ditch. Death's smile doubled! Madge knew that his life would change. Like a man let loose from a body stiffening shock of electric, Madge relaxed, returned his eyes to the place where the owl was perched, and smiled. The owl dropped its gaze, turned to the right, spread its wings, and over the muted protest of disturbed air ascended out of the woods and out of sight. Madge picked up the skull, embraced it to himself, and knelt before the hole as if in prayer. He spoke words he didn't understand. His last word, a single word sentence, declarative and threatening, Madge would never forget - "Wendigo!"

Chapter Eleven

Reed was exhausted when he returned to the house. Dawn was approaching, and the semi-darkness lingered into the morning. Reed needed to sleep if he were to be of any help to the sheriff in his search for the other child's body. He climbed the stairs to the tank room and tumbled into bed without removing his clothes. He quickly fell into a half-sleep. Immediately, his face became contorted, and he dreamed.

Reed was awakened by an anxious stirring in him. It was still dark. When he moved to sit on the edge of the bed he had a feeling that his feet could not reach the floor. He looked to the right and slowly turned his head back to the left. As he did so the panorama in front of him began to lighten. He was no longer looking at the walls of the tank room. He saw the walls and the end of a dirt tunnel. It was not a bright light that was visible at the opening. Above Reed could see that the sky was gray and darkening. In spite of the strangeness, Reed was not afraid. After the slow perusal of the scene in front of him, Reed looked down. Then the fear came! Where he had expected to see his unclad feet, he saw the gray, dirt-stained ribcage of a human skeleton. Nothing was familiar. From just below his chin to the claws of his feet, he saw a soft and fluttering coat of feathers. His talon-like feet firmly grasped two ribs of the skeleton. Reed spun out of control. He raised his arms, released his grip on the ribcage, and lifted himself toward the opening. Suddenly he was flying, high above the darkening woods and fields beneath. Everything underneath flashed rapidly by, but he could see like he had never seen before. With a single thought, Reed could slow the passing scene or brighten it. It was like he had two buttons in the back of his head; one to focus and one to tune whatever he saw. A radar-like sense of direction made it possible for him to sail through the air inside a thickly wooded forest and yet avoid crashing into the trees. He quickly broke out of the woods, surveyed the fields below, and adjusted his trajectory to the next set of woods two miles in front of him. Whatever creature body he now occupied, Reed was conscious that he was looking for something. He flew into the woods. Again he dodged and soared past the variety of trees and came to rest in a large elm standing along the side bordered by the road. As he perched high on a branch of the elm, he looked straight down to see a man dressed in dark clothes, curled into a ball, and sleeping under the thick screen of brush. When Reed surveyed the roadside along the edge of the woods, he saw another human creature. However, this body was not sleeping. This body was carrion. Most of it was hidden in a culvert of the ditch. Only the head protruded. Reed could see clearly that it was the body of a young girl. Her skin was pale and the features of the child's face were beginning to disappear because of swelling. Reed heard something. He looked below. In the underbrush, the man dressed in black was awakening. He moved from the curled prone position to sitting on the ground. His hands explored his bare head removing dirt and twigs that had stuck to his head during his sleep. Within a few seconds, the man stood, spread his arms outward into a morning stretch and yawn, and half turned his body so that Reed could see his face for the first time. Two things happened at once. Reed was stunned by the face. It was his human face. He was terrified by the fact that the man who spent the night guarding his kill in the culvert had Reed Shillinger's human face. The second was that he had lost his grip on the branch high in the elm tree. Reed tried frantically to retrieve his perch. It was impossible. So he spread his arms. He had flown to this place from a hole more than two miles away so he would fly back. He spread his arms, but they no longer supported his body in the air. He felt heavy and rather than the graceful feeling of gliding that he experienced earlier, he was tumbling toward the ground. Darkness slammed around him. He could no longer see. He was falling. As he tumbled one last time before he crashed into the ground, everything became dark. The scene in the woods disappeared.

Reed was lying there in his bed, staring at the ceiling. He raised his hands above him, noted that they were featherless and unharmed, and he took a deep breath. Reed comforted himself with an inventory of the real world of the tank room. It was daylight. He stared hopefully at the small window in the wall, carefully read the decaying label embossed on the side of the tank, and checked to see that his clothes were still in a pile near the doorway. As his mind turned to the world outside the tank room, Reed trembled. He knew that he needed to call the sheriff one more time. This time he would report that the body of the child, carried by the man in black, could be found stuffed in a culvert on the road north of the farmhouse. Then Reed became frightened. The dream had given him information that would be helpful to the investigation of the murder of the Kreutzers, but could he give the sheriff the rest of the information? Could he tell the sheriff the face he saw on the man dressed in black?

Reed decided to check the accuracy of the dream. He walked resolutely to the pile of clothes in the room, dressed, and, with shoes in hand, descended the stairs.

He switched on the lights to the old kitchen. Reed shook off the trance-like stare that had overcome him as he entered the kitchen and sat down on one of the wobbly wooden chairs to put on his shoes. As he leaned over to tie the laces, he heard a sound coming from the front porch of the house. He went to the windows in the front of the house. In the dim light, Reed saw nothing. The porch was quiet and deserted. He ran to the side door, opened it, and raced down the three steps to the lawn. He searched the lane to the left and right, scanned the farm buildings across the lane, and looked westward. He saw nothing. It was like standing on the brink of the first exploration of an uninhabited planet. For Reed the deserted place was inside himself not out there in London and Exeter townships. Once more the grayness overcame him. He felt alone and decaying. As he turned to reenter the house he quickly reminded himself that he had left a wife and two children back in Texas. Nothing supernatural had snatched them away. His journey from Texas to Michigan was not a kind of "beaming up" that happened to a fictional space traveler. He had created this loneliness. He alone had chosen this isolating journey. He had chosen to be standing on the rickety porch of his old place caught up in the tragedy of senseless murders. Whatever loneliness he felt, whatever separation from the real world, Reed had brought it on himself. He opened the door, closed it behind, and leaned disconsolately on the doorframe.

His self-condemnation had been interrupted by another thought, even an image. It was triggered by the sound on the porch. He remembered a time when the sun was shining over London Township. Sam and Daisy lived there with their two children. It was a time when Sam farmed the place, but without the advantage of modern technology. Sam had driven off to Maybee with the tractor and trailer to bring a load of cow feed from the mill. He left in the early morning and was not to return until evening. Reed remembered. The old phone on the wall in the kitchen rang three times; two longs and a short. That was the Shillinger signal. He could not remember his phone number in Texas, but the old Michigan Bell system of short and long rings from his childhood days. Daisy moved quickly to the phone. "Hello!" she announced. "Yes. Yes. When? Are you O.K?" she quizzed. "Are you sure? How do you know he's coming here?" fear was rising in her voice. "Thank you for calling, Millie. I'll call you later," Daisy said as she returned the earpiece to its hook on the side of the telephone box. Then Daisy began to move. There was a look of intensity on her face as she took him by the shoulders and gently pushed him toward the front bedroom. "Go to mommy and daddy's bedroom, Reedie! I'm getting your brother and sister, and I'll join you right away," she said as she turned toward the back door to call the other two children. Reed ran to the bedroom. He hesitated in front of the slightly open door. Normally he would not enter this room without being invited. His instinct to wait for the voice from the inside held him momentarily before he pushed the door. As he sat on the edge of Sam and Daisy's bed, he heard the sound of the others running through the house. They burst into the room. "Quickly, into the closet!" whispered Daisy. The children were like robots. They scuttled to the closet. Daisy stepped over and around them, squatted in the corner, and drew the three small children into her arms. They waited. Very soon they heard the sound of footsteps on the wrap around porch. Daisy wrapped her arms around the children, pulled them tight to herself, and let out a long breath. "Don't say a word. Don't move!" she hissed. They heard the footsteps walking the porch to the corner where it turned to connect with the door in the front of the house. Reed could see the front window of the bedroom through a gap between two of Sam's flannel shirts. The shadow of the visitor preceded him past the window. Reed sprang from Daisy's grasp and crawled toward the window. As Reed pressed against the wall next to the window, he turned to peer through the slight gap between the shade and the window frame. He could see the porch and the lawn stretching from the steps to the road. As his eyes adjusted to the brightness outside, a face leaped into view outside the window. The man was trying to see into the house. When he heard the footsteps, Reed silently moved to a new vantage point. He saw the man descending the steps to the lawn. It was then he saw the knife. Stuck through the man's belt with the handle pointed toward his right shoulder was a long vintner's knife. The handle was about eight inches long with a blade that was a foot to eighteen inches long. The blade was bright from repeated sharpening, an inch and a half wide, and the last three inches of the blade was a sharp curve coming to a point so radical that it looked like a hook. Reed gasped and rolled away from the window. The man with the knife could have easily seen them. And then what? Reed smiled. He imagined a short film clip of the escape of Reed Shillinger. He was sure a major close call had just happened. Something, fate or God, had good feelings toward Reed. The little boy crouched in that bedroom that day knew that his life was charmed. That feeling stayed with Reed for the rest of his life. Unfortunately, he made every possible effort to challenge the charm. In the days since his second stay at the Day Road farm, Reed was beginning to feel the charm slip away.

Six months after he returned to Michigan, Reed heard from his wife. Unknown to her, he knew most of what was going on in her life. There were the weekly letters from the children. Evelyn was not having the same problem that Reed had getting her life on track again.

In the beginning he was referred to as "the man." Within weeks, the letters often mentioned that "the man" was around the house when they got up to go to school in the morning. From the most recent letters the children told of a growing affection and respect for Russell (as he was now called). Reed was not surprised, though saddened, by Evelyn's speedy recovery.

The letter from Evie shocked Reed. She informed Reed that within days he would be receiving papers for the dissolution of the marriage. She told Reed that immediately after he left she began to work with their attorney to assess the value of their property. Everything was arbitrarily divided in half. The children would stay with her. The first sign of Evelyn's bitterness came when she wrote, "I'm sure that you will not want the burden of their problems growing up. You should know that anytime you decide to visit them, I will not place any obstacles in your way." That was just like Evelyn. Reed never understood how one human being could be so infinitely rational and capable of setting aside the most common emotions. Anger. Affection. She had emotions and she did reveal them. But she had the dexterity to choose the right time to display them. She could plan their appearance. Her explosive bursts of anger, her refreshing turns to affection, and her reasonable attempts to compliment and catalog Reed's strong characteristics were moments that seemed contrived.

Their marriage would end in this planned and rational way. Reed thought about disrupting Evelyn's peaceful end to twenty years of intimacy. He could hire his own lawyer and contest everything. Reed shook his head, thinking to himself. "You just can't stand it when she gets to do it her way, can you? You are the worst asshole!" he said. He took a deep breath and dropped the letter on the kitchen table. He had what he knew he needed. The day that Reed walked out of his Texas life, he was seeking the freedom of irresponsibility. Evelyn's letter was the objective assessment he wanted to hear. He was free and unattached. Reed knew that he should feel sad. But he didn't.

Chapter Twelve

Reed sat at the table in the kitchen waiting for the water on the stove to boil. Though completely still and immobile, Reed was exercising one of his perfected skills. He could sit or stand absolutely still, do nothing, for what to most people was an interminable amount of time. The lack of activity was the perfect deception because underneath his imagination would be racing. As he sat in the kitchen that morning he imagined a soap opera style plot to the rest of his life. While the choices he made often seemed clumsy and cowardly, his imagined version was always rich with courage and magic. He was about to complete the prologue to his theater of the mind when he heard steps on the porch outside the kitchen. Reed moved to the door and was relieved when he saw the flat-brimmed shadow of a trooper's hat through the glass of the door.

"Mr. Shillinger?" he announced. Reed nodded. "I'd like you to come with me this morning. We thought that we might search your property to begin with. If there is a corpse of a young girl to be found, we will need to start here where the killer was last seen. We just need you to show us where you last saw him, and you might be able to help us look in the most likely places first."

Reed answered but with the caution needed to cover his recollection of the owl dream in the night. "I'll help as much as I can. Let me get my jacket. I'll be right out."

The two men walked together to a four-wheel drive vehicle. Reed directed him to the space between the woodshed and the granary leading down the slope to the lane. When they approached the granary, Reed began to narrate the events preceding the chase just before getting caught on the barb wire fence. He said that he was sure that the killer had escaped into the woods. The more he talked, the more cautious he became in covering the images of his dream. They would find the body of the little girl in the culvert, but he was determined to show that his knowledge was pure logic followed by pure luck. The vehicle bounced across the rickety wooden bridge over the ditch, slowly climbed the slope to the level ground, and proceeded down the lane toward the woods. At several points the trooper stopped the car and, on foot, examined the ground in the fields next to the lane. "I need to make sure that he came this way. I haven't seen tracks on the lane, so he must have walked through the fields." he said as he pulled the fence lines apart and stepped through. For several minutes the trooper examined the ground. Stooping, he pulled the dry grass apart. "Sure enough! He came this way. I've found a footprint. My guess is that he was heading for those woods. He needed cover in the approaching daylight. I think we'll see something once we get into that woods." he declared.

There were signs of an old logging road cutting through the woods. Again, the trooper stopped the vehicle at one point and searched the area on foot. This time Reed joined the officer. As he wandered in a large circle in the woods, he carefully watched the ground hoping that he would see evidence that the killer had passed through this section of the forest. His elation was just as sincere, however, when the trooper shouted, "Hey! Shillinger! Come over here and see this!" The trooper was hunched over something in the brush. He reached down with a pen in his hand and picked up a bloody piece of cloth from the ground. It looked like a child's sock. "I'm afraid that we're on the right track here. I'm not going to like what we are about to see. There are some tracks here. He headed in that direction. Toward the road over there. Let's drive over that way." he said.

Reed sat nervously in the Jeep as they zigzagged through the rest of the woods. He was delighted when they stopped before crossing the ditch on to the road. The culvert was only twenty feet to the right, and, if he feigned a casual glance to the right, Reed was sure that he would be able to see the body of the girl protruding from the end of the culvert. He turned his head. Both Reed and the trooper saw the bird eject itself from the ditch. "I'll be damned! An owl in broad daylight! I've never seen such a thing. Look! He has something in his claws." Reed listened and watched. The owl lurched to the road level with a piece of cloth in his talon. With a glance, he took in the Jeep and launched himself into the sky. The trooper slammed the accelerator to the floor and was over the place which the bird had just vacated. He fell from the vehicle in his rush to inspect the ditch. There was a frantic quickness in his motions until he looked over the berm of the road. Then he froze. Reed opened the car door in time to hear the trooper exclaim, "My God! She's here. I need to call the coroner and the sheriff. The bastard stuffed her in the culvert." Reed was not ready for his own reaction. He did not move out of his sliding exit from the car. With one foot on the ground and the other still inside the cab, he crumbled against the back of the seat in horror. He had been so preoccupied with protecting himself that he had not anticipated the numbing shock of a horrible dream coming true to detail. And it was an owl that had pinpointed the location for the trooper!

Reed was still sitting in that stunned position when he heard the trooper on the radio calling for the coroner. His encounter with the murderer the night before, the discovery of the bodies in the well, and now the body of the girl found exactly where he had seen it in his dream: all of this pushed Reed into the deepest darkness of his entire life. As he sat, half in the Jeep and half out, Reed was overcome by a deep sadness. Instinctively, he pushed himself away from the trooper's car and began to walk through the woods toward the house. He had no need to see the body. After all he had seen it from the sky.

Chapter Thirteen

He walked quickly. He could feel within himself the driving need to heal. There was no guarantee that anything could rescue him from the pit that the past few days had dug for him. Yet there was a life force that couldn't be denied. He made the ten or fifteen minute walk to the house without losing his resolve. Before the day was over he would see Caren. After a shower and coffee Reed went through his yet unpacked extra suitcase until he found his other pair of jeans and the only new thing he owned - a flannel shirt, still in the folds and carrying the pins from the manufacturer. He dressed and left the house. It didn't matter that it was still early morning and that schools everywhere had not yet opened. He drove to Grapestown School. The radio was playing an old Elvis song. He couldn't remember what it was called, but, because the tune was rustled from the American folk past, it was familiar. Forty five minutes later as he watched from the far corner of the school's parking lot, he saw Caren drive into the lot. Before she had stopped the engine, he was approaching her car. He feared that his eagerness would frighten her, so he changed his walk, took some intensity and eagerness out of it, and pasted a smile on his face. She didn't notice him until he was next to her. "Good morning." he ventured. At the sound of his voice Caren stiffened, and an armload of books tumbled to the pavement. "Jesus, Reed! You nearly scared the shit out of me!" There was an edge to her voice. At the same time Reed saw a momentary smile as she snatched the books one at a time from the ground. As she stooped, Reed was surprised by a physical longing within himself as he watched the tightening of her skirt against her hips. It had been months. He joined Caren in retrieving the books and began to make excuses for being there at such a strange hour. "I didn't know where you lived or what your phone number was, so I decided to try to meet you at the one place where I knew you would be. A little compulsive, right?"

Each word tumbled from his mouth a little faster than the last. He sounded like a man afraid to stop lest he loose his courage and run for a convenient hiding place.

"Will you go out with me? To dinner? A movie?"

Caren never stopped reloading her books from the pavement. She looked straight ahead as a slight expression of amusement appeared on her face.

She turned to Reed, "When? Reed? Stop talking Reed. I'm trying to say 'yes.'"

Reed spoke ten more words, each one coming at a longer interval from the other. Then silence. Reed suddenly felt very different. He realized how alone he had been for the past month. Reed enjoyed the first two weeks. Two weeks as a hermit was enough!

When he heard the word "yes" out of Caren's mouth, something began to sing inside him; maybe it was more like a cat's purr, a sound of peacefulness and contentment. Caren took three quick steps toward the entrance of the building before a memory rocketed to the present and would not be denied.

"Reed? Do you want to hear something strange?" she asked.

Reed was still checking all his vital functions so he nodded just to keep her talking and close.

"The way you were. Just now when you asked me. That happened before. Remember? When you asked me to the Junior-Senior Prom, our first date. I was standing at my locker stuffing in a pile of books. You stood next to me, staring at my profile, and refusing to say 'hello' or to let me talk. When you were finally able to ask me to the prom, I figured then you might stop talking so I said I would go. You never said a word, just turned, and walked away."

Caren shook her head and looked surprised. Before Reed could answer she was on the steps of the school building with her hand on the door. He ran to her. She handed him a card with her name, address, and phone number.

"Six tonight? I'll pick you up." he announced.

When he saw her nod, he ran to his truck waving to her as he went. There was something warm for a change, something to dream - something alive to dream.

After Reed left the school parking lot he turned to the east. He was heading toward the Seitz tavern to ask about the people who lived near Day Road. When he left the farm that morning he had a plan for his life, at least a plan for a day of that life.

As he got out of the truck, he saw Uncle Harry standing in the doorway of the tool shed. Harry was a retired municipal judge. Harry Shillinger had been born on a farm, managed to escape to a university education, and eventually law school, and the passing of the bar exam provided him with a permanent protective shield from the creeping return of the Shillinger family curse; that is, to die in a farmhouse somewhere in the cloudy environs of London or Exeter townships. Reed laughed at the irony of it. Harry stood in the doorway of the ancient shed wearing a pair of very large "bib" overalls, looking very much like the typical native of London and Exeter. Harry's "escape" from his origins was pre-ordained to fail. In spite of all efforts, Uncle Harry would probably die of old age, dressed in the typical costume of a Michigan farmer, alone in the dark countryside of southeastern Michigan.

The old man was standing in the entrance to the shed.

"Good morning, Uncle Harry. Remember me?" he shouted across the interval of several feet.

"Morning. You look familiar but I can't figure what your name might be. You must be related. You have the right build and the nose gives you away." Harry observed.

As he came within arm's reach, Reed held out his hand, "Reed Shillinger, Uncle Harry. Sam and Daisy's son." announcing this information gave Reed a sense of relief. Now he could get on with the reason for his visit.

"I've moved back to the farm on Day Road. I don't own it, but I live there and take care of it. Two nights ago someone killed four of the Kreutzers. He killed the mother, the daughters, and the father. The son survived. Anyway, the police are looking for a man with a very dark countenance, wearing dark clothes, strong enough to run while carrying a dead body, and probably living somewhere in the vicinity. You've been around here all your life, Uncle Harry, is there someone who could be doing such things?" Reed wanted to say it all before he was quizzed about why he was living on the old farm after all these years of being away. It worked. Harry started talking immediately about events of equal mystery from years past.

"There haven't been that many murders around here, but some deaths have been declared suicides, and, even at that, the coroner was reluctant many times to write the "s" word on the certificate. During the fifties, there were probably ten strange deaths in the area. People who lived alone were a little isolated by the location of the farm they owned, and were elderly. The one I remember best came right after old Carl Smith hung himself from a coat hook in his niece's closet. You must have been a small boy when this happened."

"I remember this one because I was a prosecutor at that time, and we came that close to actually having a case against someone. Of course, the fact that we couldn't come up with that "someone" was the main reason we didn't proceed. Another victim lived on Muehliesen Road near where it crosses Day. They found him hanging by the neck from a thin rafter in his corn crib. I'll never forget it. The sheriff left him hanging until I could see the crime scene. When I opened the door of the crib, I saw rats scampering from the inside into the corn and through the slats of the outside walls. The sun was up so there were stripes of light slanting across the blue face of old man Laufenberg. There was no wind, but, for some reason, the body was swinging slightly. On the side of the old man's head there was a slight gash with dried blood covering it. We were sure that someone had knocked him unconscious and then strung him up. The sheriff pointed out that there had been only one set of footprints in the mud at the entrance to the crib. He walked up to the swinging corpse and drew his finger along the length of rope starting at the knot that fastened it to the rafter above the head of the dead man. You could see evidence of mud and fragments of dry leaves stuck to the rope.

It appeared that the rope had been dragged through the mud for a pretty good distance. What was most puzzling was the fact that one of the leaf fragments stuck to the mud was an oak leaf. There were no oak trees on Laufenberg's farm. That rope had to have been dragged through the mud somewhere far away from that corncrib." Harry was shaking his head. The incident still perplexed him. Reed, on the other hand, was turning white and stiff as Harry told the story. A memory flashed through his mind. He saw the rope bouncing along the ground in the woods behind the Day Road place. He felt the prickles of fear rising up his right side and creeping behind his ear and disappearing under his hairline.

"Harry? Would that have happened about the time Dad and Mom moved away from the farm?"

Harry's answer was sure, "Yeah. Just before. I remember helping them with the paper work on their move and talking about the Laufenberg case with them. As I said, you couldn't have been more than four or five years old."

Reed could not decide whether hearing of a nightmare from the mouth of someone who never had seen it was reassuring or frightening. For the first time since the nightmare had premiered inside his sleeping mind, Reed was curious. The next time the dream occurred he would try to remember the details. The dream had to be connected with something that he had actually seen. When he visited Sam and Daisy he would ask them about times he might have wandered toward the woods at the back of the farm.

"You know, Reed", Harry trying to regain Reed's attention, "It always looked to me that all the farmers around the old place were content to ignore the stuff that was going on in those days. And from what I heard happened the other day, they're still ignoring it."

"What do you mean, Harry?" Reed was experiencing some rekindling of interest in Harry's ongoing account.

Harry had a question for Reed, but he didn't ask it.

"Look at it yourself. One time I counted six suicides and two murders that happened within two or three miles of that farm in the period of 20 years. I keep wondering why someone hasn't figured out that 8 mysterious deaths in one county in 20 years is unusual enough, let alone in one tiny corner of a county. As it is the farmers there shake their heads and mumble something about how terrible people can be to each other."

Harry was shaking his head when he changed the subject. "How's the family, Reed? Those kids must be in school by now. Did you and your wife put them in Monroe or Dundee schools?"

Reed still was not comfortable when he talked about the disaster of his marriage, but with Harry he practiced an air of objectivity as he spoke.

"My wife and I are separated, and it looks like they are going to stay in Texas. I haven't seen the kids for several weeks now. Evelyn has sued me for a divorce. I'm not quite as settled as I would like to be right now, Harry. I haven't figured out what I'm going to do."

Harry didn't answer. He put his hand on his shoulder as Reed turned to walk toward the truck. Both of them knew that their conversation had already ventured too far into the personal for people with Shillinger blood in their veins. Reed needed to retreat and Harry was hungry. They walked together to the truck, shook hands and, without second glances, left each other. It was the way of the men in the family. They were equally comfortable; talking with each other or alone with their thoughts and dreams. The Shillinger men seldom made the connection between the pain inside and the fact that they spent much of their lives in solitary self-absorption.

On the drive back to the farm, Reed was surprised by his high spirits. He didn't take long figuring out the reason. For the first time since his return to London township, Reed was about to have an extended conversation with someone other than the police, grocery clerks, or his parents. But he also began to feel the uncertainty that preceded intimacy. Would Caren feel the same way? This was not the ordinary kind of date. Two people were about to roll the dice with two lives. Although totally separate, they had met by accident, and, to add a touch of comedy, they had been "baby" boyfriend and girlfriend in the past. While searching for a shirt that was clean and wrinkle-free, Reed thought about the different ways he could make a fool of himself. He could not remember the last time he was afraid of being alone with a woman. He could not remember the last time he joined another person in feelings and sensations deeply personal. Two antagonistic emotions fought for control of Reed Shillinger - fear and childlike exuberance.

EXUBERANCE WON!

Caren and Reed were sitting across from each other in the booth of diner when Reed noticed once again what it was about Caren that filled him with yearning. She was talking about her children. Her eyes were windows; a soft blue-green with a slight turn upward as the line of the lashes followed the turn toward her temples. Caren never used make-up on her eyes. The eyebrows were soft and complimented her facial lines. Her eyes were inviting and gentle. When she laughed the eyes danced. When sadness came, her eyes moistened, but never darkened. Reed remembered her angry. She would look down. Her eyes retained their softness and brightness. When angry she simply shut herself off from those around her. As she spoke, she touched the area around her eyes. Her words were suddenly detached from her thoughts. A puzzled smile hurried across the lower part of her face. In mid-sentence she stopped, reached for Reeds' arm, and asked, "Why are you staring at my eyes? Do I have a loose lash or something?"

He had been discovered, "You caught me! I was watching your eyes because I can't help it. Back in high school your eyes always won over the guys."

"Alright. I'll accept that. The last time a man told me that there was something that was noticeable about me. . ." As she spoke she slowly withdrew her hand from his arm. If he had been paying attention he would have noticed that in taking her hand away she was inviting him to prepare for a touch more intimate, more exciting. Reed missed it, or he was afraid of it. He changed the subject. "Caren, have you heard about the strange goings-on around the place where I'm living? About the killings?"

She reluctantly joined him, "I read about it in the News. It's horrible. Is that house near you?"

"I discovered it. After we met at the river. I found a man skulking around the buildings. He was carrying the little girl. When I went across the road to call the police at Kreutzers, their house had been broken into, and everybody except the boy dead."

"Do they have an idea who did it?" Caren asked.

Reed told more than he had planned, "They are sure that it was done by someone who lives nearby. He doesn't have a car. He knows the area well. And the police are hoping to connect other strange tragedies with this person. Did you know that in the past few years there have been a lot of strange deaths within two or three miles of my place? Most of them have been officially categorized as suicides, but now everyone is beginning to wonder."

There was a pause in the conversation. Caren was not going to hear more of this event. She said, "It sounds as if you are right in the middle of this thing. I hope you're safe. It must be lonely. Of course, you have always done well alone. But is it secure? Aren't you afraid?"

"I haven't been. The deaths were always children, old men, and the parents of the children who most likely were in the way. To be honest, I've started locking the door at night and when I leave the house. It is not that it will do much good. There are probably ten ways to get in. This killer has been around. He seems to know everything there is to know about most of the places in London. I have other reasons to be afraid; reasons that have nothing to do with these murders."

"What are you talking about, Reed? Are you in trouble?" Caren asked with a look of shock and concern on her face.

"For a long time I have been restless. I kept my job. Did well at it, but I tried other things. Nothing seemed to hold my attention very long. Sure, I did everything well. I even managed to be a husband determined to keep the marriage going. But Evelyn needed me to keep my promise that our marriage would never be average. That's what happened to us. We allowed average! My decision to come back here was my desperate hope to find the extraordinary; in myself and in others. Evelyn had already found the extraordinary. In someone else.

I don't blame her. Much longer, waiting for me to restart, and she would have become like me. Totally burned out!"

"Have you found it? Have you found the extraordinary?" She asked because she was afraid he might quit talking.

"I'm still looking." He paused as her face and eyes silenced his voice, "I may be close. But I need to find it in myself. I hope you understand. I'm afraid to be analytical."

There was a long silence between them. Caren looked at the half-eaten plate of food in front of her and moved slightly in her chair. Reed stared at her face searching for some indication that she might bolt and run away. As he stared at her, he was thinking about a different problem. Reed was afraid he had said too much; that once again he had spoken to reveal too much of the darkness within himself. He thought of Evelyn. Her strength was very important early in their relationship. She was not afraid of Reed's dark spirit. He could tell her of his fear, of the anonymous and surreptitious bogey men inside him, and she would never blink. She was the first person who didn't run away. So he waited. Caren's stillness finally spelled out what he most feared to acknowledge. The one who would listen to him and stand with him was yet to be found. He dropped his eyes to his plate. After a few seconds Caren moved; her chair sliding away from the table. "She's actually leaving! I guess I miscalculated that one!" he thought. As he was about to say good-bye, he felt her close to his side. She leaned over, gently held him with her hands on his shoulders, and whispered in his ear. "Let's go, Reed. Take me somewhere with you. Darkness is kind. Love grows there."

Chapter Fourteen

Nothing was said between them as they drove to the farmhouse. Reed was comfortable with the silence. When he slid behind the wheel of the truck, Caren reached for his arm and pulled herself to his side. He could feel the length of her; the curve of her thighs against his, the softness of her hips, and the tempting and elusive beckoning from the gentle pressure of her breast. He sensed the question and the promise. Without speaking he experimented with an answer and wondered about the wisdom of a promise in return. There was no way to say it! So he allowed his body to go to her. As he turned off the key of the truck in the driveway, Reed found her lips and gently kissed her. It was his invitation, his promise.

Reed led the way through the kitchen and into the dining room of the old house. Even though Caren walked behind him he could feel her wrapped around him. The bare bulb in the center of the room was enough to light every corner of the house. The glaring light spilled into the living room and fell on one end of the old couch. There was no other furniture in the room. The dining room was impoverished. In the past events of great celebration and noble joy had taken place in that room. The wallpaper curled away from meeting points in the corners and puckered away from seams successively around the room. Stains here and there were like scattered liver spots mixed among numerous purplish bruises on the body of a battered transient. But this was a house not a man. Reed remembered the real person with him in the room. The bulb became the sun in the center of a limited universe. He was gliding through it to another place, but here, before the two them touched Reed would speak to Caren of hopes and expectations. He circled the room staying far way from the light. He brushed his hand against the table in front of the window. When his hand was obstructed by a cardboard box sitting there, he patted the contents and clutched the blanket that filled the box. He turned. He leaned against the post of the double wide entrance into the living room. He held the blanket tight to his chest like an anxious child. He tossed the blanket across the room. He turned to Caren, leaned and braced himself with a forearm on the entrance arch. Nothing helped. At last, Caren was standing near him.

"Reed, forget how close we were before. That was a long time ago. We were children then. I want to be close to you now, to make love to you. No guessing. No games." she said.

There was no game played during their lovemaking. For Reed, making love usually resulted in a loser and a winner. Neither he nor Caren intended to win or feared losing that night. They embraced each other and touched each other with the intent that both would experience small, scattered, and numerous rushes of ecstasy. Caren walked into his arms with her hands forward. When she put the ends of her fingers to the top button of his shirt, he experienced a chill of anticipation. His hands reached for her waist. He felt her curving softness through the fabric of her sweater. He slowly worked his hands under her sweater and raised it. The drama had begun. The curtain was about to rise revealing an offering of emotion and action directed and staged for the joy of another. The actors were ready. The cues carefully spoken. The eye contact ultimately essential. Caren and Reed found each other that night; searching deep within the other, seeking the excitement of newness and knowledge, they found themselves. Like a wave that slides along a long stretch of beach crashing here, then crashing there, and transforming its touch on the sand into a caress, the lovers caressed and exploded, giving and receiving.

Later, when they quietly held each other, remembering , Caren said, "Will you regret this in the morning?"

"Regret? I'll regret that we can't be together every hour of every day." he answered.

Reed stared through the wide doorway into the dining room. The light from the kitchen flowed over

Caren where she was curled in his arms half covered with the blanket. Reed could feel it happening again: that feeling of unworthiness. A tear gathered on the brim of his eyelid.

"Are you alright?" she asked, "Are you thinking this will end? Did I do something wrong?"

"Wrong? No. Something wonderful and generous."

As he spoke Caren turned toward him. She searched his face for signs to go with the tears. There were none. Someday she would accept that Reed's melancholia came from a remote corner of his being. Faraway in his subconscious was the memory of something hurtful – forgetfulness it's only cure. The blanket slipped from Caren's shoulders. His eyes followed the line of her neck and jaw line to her eyes. There he stopped until receiving permission to move on. He smiled when he looked at her mouth. Without hesitation he gazed at her breasts. He felt full and refreshed. Caren disguised her sensuality in the conservative dress of a Midwestern housewife. Sometimes she wore the costume of a professional, a Midwestern elementary schoolteacher. The sight of her was sunshine on a spring day in southeastern Michigan. Her searching eyes were like the warm and fleeting rays of the sun. Then he closed his eyes to hold the vision. Caren noticed.

"Reed, tell me what you're thinking." a shadow came over her face as she pulled the blanket up to cover herself. "I want us to be closer. Why do you retreat into yourself at exactly the moment you're ready to open up, at exactly the moment I let you into my life?"

Reed knew what she meant. "Caren, I came back here to take a final step. To survive! I'm not sure how I knew that. Over the last few years, the view I have of the world has changed. I compare it to waking up to a bright spring day; full of expectations, only to have it cloud over by midmorning, the wind turn cold, and flurries in the air before dusk. I have tried to control the grayness. I have tried to push it away. It never works. When I describe it to my friends or to Evelyn, someone always gets around to calling it my mid-life crisis. Naming it is a good way to bring an uncomfortable conversation to a close. But it isn't the answer for me."

She leaned into him and slipped her arms around his waist, snuggling. A look of concern was on her face for one moment, but like a wisp of cloud it passed quickly.

"Reed, I'm glad you came back. I never expected it. I never dreamed. This is a feeling I've never had before. I'll take the tomorrows." Both were silent for a long time before they fell asleep in each other's arms.

The dim light in the old living room was enough for the watcher to see their faces. The light also cast unnatural shadows. The north side of the house was nothing but a black hulk with the rectangular viewfinder window that framed the entwined lovers, covered and sleeping on the old couch. A slight wind had arisen about halfway to midnight. Clouds began to secretly spread over London Township; slithering and sliding over the world below, soundless and unnoticed by all the inhabitants except the night creatures. There was no source of light, yet somehow in the blackness a shadow appeared on the side of the house near the window that framed Reed and Caren's hopeful beginning. The shadow moved along the wall of the house sliding periodically behind a spirea bush. When the specter came near the edge of the light, it paused, turned away, and then stood squarely in front of the window challenging the light. Through the glass, Madge saw his next victim. When one of them moved Madge slipped into the darkness. The vision had been enough for now. A thrill went through Madge as he contemplated his next task; the next sacrifice. After backing quietly out of the light that spilled from the window, Madge walked away. There was just enough light striking the blade inserted in his belt that inside the house, Reed was awakened by a nearly imperceptible flash of light racing across the wall in front of him. The light was gone before Reed had time to think about what it meant. His thoughts were quickly absorbed in the events of the night. He whispered under his breath, "I can let go of the past. It's the past that refuses to let go of me."

Chapter Fifteen

Soon after the couple inside awoke. It was late, so the dirt roads which were normally deserted in the daytime were desolate. The lights of the truck bounced, the beams lengthening and shortening with each chuckhole in the road. Since returning to Michigan, Reed had learned to drive like the proverbial "Sunday afternoon" driver. It was a necessity. Most of the roads in southeastern Michigan were narrow, high-crowned two-lane county roads. Two interstates passed through the fringes of Monroe County. Otherwise, the number of paved roads fairly equaled the number of roads that had never been paved. Driving on the dirt roads required concentration. Especially from late fall through the late spring the dirt roads developed ever-growing chuckholes. Drivers were required to tightrope around the holes or adjust the speed of the vehicle so that the unavoidable hole would not permanently damage tires or suspension apparatus. Between the farm and the city where Caren lived were several miles of this hazardous roadway. Reed was almost grateful for the opportunity to concentrate on the driving to avoid the obvious silence that had developed between the two of them since they had left the farmhouse. There was a gnawing discomfort in the pit of Reed's stomach. The feeling started the moment Caren had wrapped her arms around him on the couch in the old house. It had been a long time since he had experienced the anxiety that came with the dawn of passion and affection. He often wondered if everyone who wanted to be in love had the same fear. It came when he wanted to lose himself in the life of another, to discover once and for all the fullness of another's being. But for now, he was grateful that once again he was alive under his skin.

Caren said nothing at first. When the truck bounced on to the high pavement of the secondary road leading into Monroe, she moved her hand from the seat beside her to Reed's muscular shoulder. Something like an electric shock stunned Reed. There was a sound inside his head like static exploding. He turned to look at her. She searched his eyes. When their gazes locked into each other's, Reed stopped the truck. It was time to talk. Reed knew it, and Caren was prepared for it.

"Reed, it's been a long time since I had the faintest hope that I could love a man," she was pausing for breaths between the words, "So it's frightening and, at the same time, thrilling to experience what I am feeling now."

"I know." said Reed, "I have had this terrible knot in my gut for the last two hours. The only time it went away was when I held you in my arms back at the house. It was like standing close to the edge of a steep precipice, knowing that to get too close would to be drawn over the edge, not by the force from behind me, but a force within me.

"Reed," she pronounced his name slowly, filling it with whole thoughts, "You have always filled every word, every look, and every emotion with a lifetime of meaning. If I embrace you, it's not a pay-off, it's a promise."

Reed laughed at himself and moved over toward her. "No one has ever promised me anything," he paused for a thought that ambushed him in mid-sentence, "That may not be true. I could never accept the open-endedness of a promise. Such gifts frighten me. I'm never sure that I have the right gift to reciprocate."

Caren put her hands above Reed's shoulders, encircled the back of his head, and drew his mouth to hers. He felt the promise of her. The power of her loving him was overwhelming. Something small and foreign slipped from his eye and made a moist trail down his cheek. When Caren tilted her head back from his lips, she looked at Reed. "Take me home, Reed. I want to be close enough to you learn about you; to start a promise."

A strange light awakened Reed in the morning. The wall in front of him was filled with light. The walls to the left and to the right were impossible to see. Caren was asleep. Reed felt her power, her warmth, and the gentle pull of her - inviting. After quietly entering Caren's house upon their return the night before, Caren and Reed, anxious and anticipating the answer to the unspoken question about the durability of ancient and youthful love, stopped in the doorway of Caren's bedroom. All the promises, spoken and unspoken aside, what they were about to do was one of those no-turning-back-we-will-accept-whatever-happens actions. For Reed it was the uncharacteristic action of one who could count on one hand the times in his life when he had opened the broad gate of his emotional defenses. For Caren it was the act of one who deeply trusted the power of the gift of herself to heal both the one she loved and that part of her that was slowly dying. Caren leaned resignedly against the doorpost. Reed turned to her. In the soft light of the room, he could see Caren's eyes alight with vulnerability one moment and sparkling with volatility the next. Reed and Caren both sighed and their foreheads touched. It was like a signal for the dance to begin. Their bodies pivoted and moved to the center of the room. Each dancer put a hand on the other to caress and to seek. Their eyes met and words could be heard; gentle whispers from the core of each dancer's being. The whispers were joined by movement; once, twice, their movements surprised the other, but before long a flawless synchrony. Silence continued throughout the dance. They created a song, a silent sensuous song. There were no listeners. There was no orchestra. The scene was like a ballet where the audience was deaf. There was a rhythm. There was a moment when each dancer's individuality blurred into oneness with the other. Later, with a sudden burst of energy from each into and toward the other, the song gently ended. For Reed there came the sleep that he had not slept for years. The light across the way nudged him into wakefulness and thought. This was not his room in the gloomy house on Day Road. There was no emptiness that smothered here. There was light, Caren, and hope.

A few miles away, another man began his dance. The man stared into a thick gray cover of smoky overcast. He waited. The man waited, like a statue, for the signal to become flesh. He was certain it would come. When it came, Madge would step into the yard behind the house. There he would wait. His waiting lasted a few minutes or a few hours. Waiting was never a burden. He never was impatient or angry. Madge would stand until his body and his senses were ready. He knew that. The signal to begin came from a wise force. Each subsequent dance tuned him like an instrument. This morning in the gray dawnless sky, Madge heard the welcome sound again. A faint smile flickered at the ends of his arid and nearly hidden mouth. "Iph-Iph-Iph," "Iph-Iph-Iph." He listened. He heard the signal before he saw the sign, but he waited. The sound of wings cutting the misty air was not enough. The sign to dance was the sound and sight of the moving wide-eyed creature of darkness. Suddenly it appeared overhead. Its flight was high until it made the little turn to fly directly into Madge's view. As it did so the bird dropped in altitude and flew in a line a few feet over his head. Madge smiled. He met the stare of the creature. For a split second he looked into the eyes of his angel of freedom. He could do what he had been born to do. Madge's body began to sway, then turned, his arms lifted rhythmically from his sides, mimicking the owl that disappeared in the cloudy sky behind him. Madge was transformed into a graceful dancer. As long as the sky was gray and obscured by the thick clouds overhead, Madge would dance. When the sun appeared, he would proceed. His victim would be revealed and the bloody ritual would be completed.

As he danced, Madge remembered the man and woman in the house on Day Road. Surely the wisdom of the People would call for one of them to die. Several times this man had crossed Madge's path. There was the night behind the barn at the man's farm, the encounter on the road, and the spectacle through the living room window. Madge was always careful about these decisions. There was never a choice of victims that did not create great anxiety for Madge. His was a priestly task. The Underground People demanded his energy and wisdom. Only he could choose. There was no light from the sky or a sign from the dark world of those he served. The choice of the victim was left entirely to him. An important principle of the Underground was involved. Madge began life learning the principles of the Underground People. For those who live between the earth and sky, the Great Spirit is known in the ebb and flow of life. In this cycle death is never a tragedy. Those who die give life to those who begin life. Madge's priestly actions were offerings. Each of these offerings was his way of participating in nature's cycle. The offerings were significant because of the elite qualities each victim possessed. He decided what was elite in each one. He weighed one victim against another. He chose.

He chose Reed Shillinger. This decision was made without personal feelings. Madge saw himself as an instrument of a higher, mysterious, and inexplicable power. There was no need to defend the killings. He often recalled the day the Great Spirit assigned him the task of punishing the non-people living in the River Raisin basin.

He was thirteen years old when the old man came to him. He was sitting on the front step of the house. The front porch was one of the few cool places available to the boy that day. August in southeastern Michigan is often unpleasantly hot. An outsider might be perplexed and disturbed by the way a young boy could sit on the front porch for hours and be entertained by nothing.

The action, however, was inside the boy's mind. The sounds of the sparrows nagging each other over bits of grass and food, the argumentative dissonance of the starlings stubbornly insisting that each one had a reserved inch of the telephone wire were not inconsequential sounds to him. Everything that moved, all that changed was alive to Madge. The trees were his brothers and sisters, the birds his confidants, and the sky his home. He heard the sounds of nature; sounds which others never heard. His excitement at hearing the sounds was often treated with derisive laughter from his friends and stern rebukes from his mother and father.

As he lulled on the porch that day, he stared at the line of trees that hugged the bank of the River Raisin, a mile away. Lying on the porch with his head propped against the wall, Madge compressed his eyelids into a squint. It was a new way to see the world. He saw a flash of light in the trees along the river. In the place where the flash had been there appeared a black spot; like a tear in a water color painting of the distant forest. The tear grew in size; as if an invisible vandal were holding a lighted match against the back of the painting. He held his squint! The thought that any of this was real never entered his mind. The flash and hole were in his mind. He could stop it whenever he wanted. But the spot continued to grow and expand. For all he knew he would be covered by the increasing size of the dark spot coming toward him. It didn't happen. The dark spot flashed to white, seemed to hover for a second and gain dimension, and dropped to the ground on the other side of the tool shed on the east side of the house. Madge blinked. It was time for the vision to be gone. But when he opened his eyes, something or someone new was coming toward him. Shuffling alongside the shed was an old man.

He was dressed in black wool trousers held up by a pair of suspenders with shredded edges and a pair of leather thongs on each leg that hung from fasteners inside the waistline of the trousers. He looked like a walking scarecrow. His shirt was the cotton type that the old farmers of Exeter Township purchased every year at Helzer's store. The shirt was long-sleeved blue cotton and never seemed to wear out. The material was cool enough to wear in August, warm enough for the biting cold of January, and strong enough to protect fleshy forearms from the sharp butts of baled straw and hay. The man was short, five feet five inches at the most. His shoulders were turned slightly to the left as if going forward had more to do with throwing the right shoulder than moving the feet. He split his gaze between the ground and Madge. Madge was aware of his eyes even before he could clearly see the man's face. The old man's gaze never failed to return to Madge. The man's face changed each split second. Madge was reminded of the outdoor theater near the railroad tracks in Maybee. It never failed. There would be a tear in the film. Suddenly the picture began to flash in a jerky fashion; single still images giving the impression of the characters caught in a moment of time. The old man's face changed with each new flash. Terror took over when each new face also changed from gender to gender and youth to aging. These images returned at each of the sacrificial killings.

At this new encounter, the grown-up Madge lurched to his feet and rushed the specter coming toward him.

His arms and hands waved frantically in front of his eyes with the desperate hope that he could erase the vision. When the old man continued to advance Madge fell to the ground and buried his face in the grass.

The specter spoke. The voice cut in and out like a bad radio.

"You have done well, Chinquik! The Great Spirit has seen your service and bravery. I have come to give you one last assignment. The People need a camp. They need a place where they are free to wander without interference from the invaders and land stealers. It is here where they were born and died. It is here that they must have the freedom to join in the one great dance of the Dead Who Live. There is one yet who stands in the way. He is our enemy. You must cleanse the land. He is the invader. Are you ready?"

Madge nodded and grunted in the affirmative, digging his face deeper into the dusty, grassy earth where he fell. "I am ready! You know that!" he answered, "But who is this last enemy? Will you tell his name?"

"I will show you. You must always watch for my signal," were the last words Madge heard.

There was a long silence. Madge slowly raised his head, tipping his face forward. He saw a pair of feet clothed in a ragged pair of moccasins. He looked up until he saw the face of a person from another world. He was dressed in rags covering a bone thin body, brown, almost metallic. A whirlwind began to twist around the two of them. The whirlwind gathered sand and debris around them. Madge was lifted to his feet, and the image began to change. The man's feet were sucked into his torso. They were transformed into claw-like appendages. The body became matted with feathers, dark in color. In a burst of light, an owl appeared, hovered before his eyes, and then rocketed to the sky. Its flight was an explosion toward the east. When the sound faded the creature had disappeared into the forested fringe of the river.

Chapter Sixteen

The old judge was not obsessed with the mystery of the brutal deaths in London Township, but he thought often of the coincidences involved. Several times a day his thoughts turned to the possibilities. This time it happened while he was carelessly wandering through the stack of old papers that were on the desk near the front of the house. One of the documents that passed through his hands was the deed to the tavern. He had never really read it. So he began. The deed had passed through the hands of at least three owners before the judge owned the place. The original Shillingers had purchased the French claim in 1840. The purchase was made from the original settlers who had received the land as a grant from the French colonial administration after the initial surveys. The land was used by the Potawatami tribe for hunting, living space and some agriculture. This deed simply stated that the land, first received from the Potawatami tribe through treaty was now the possession of the Judge Harry Shillinger. At some point in time, the tract of land had been divided in half: the western half going to the judge's ancestor's brother. Subsequently, that half was divided when about eighty acres were sold to a family by the name of Majerosky. For forty years until twenty years ago, the land had been occupied by the Shillingers on either end and sandwiched between them, the Majeroskys.

The judge thought about the equation. What connected him with Reed Shillinger was one man, his last name was Majerosky. Since Reed's return to Michigan, the judge had spoken with Reed once. He knew that Reed had been involved in the discovery of the bodies at the Kreutzer place. But most telling to the judge was the land connection. So the judge decided that day to go for a ride.

The folks in this part of the world have a saying about what the judge was about to do. When they finished the evening chores, or it might be a Sunday afternoon, actually when they had become curious about the neighbor's crops and wanted to compare their own success with the neighbor's, they "went for a ride." It is likely as well that "going for a ride" was a way of showing off the new "horseless carriage" in this territory 30 miles from the Motor City. The truth is that it is very unlikely that there are people anywhere in this country who choose, on a regular basis for recreational purposes, cruising around the countryside on muddy, potholed, roads. However, as is obvious now, it wasn't the "ride," it was the inventory of the neighbor's goods and progress that provided the recreation.

The judge made a terrible choice that afternoon. His impulsive decision to turn into the driveway of the Majerosky farm was the sad beginning to a good man's ending.

Madge was working in the vineyard when the judge pulled into his place. From among the vines he could watch the approaching visitor without being seen. Madge knew the judge. At one time he had thought that he would choose the judge as one of the sacrifices. The coming of the younger Shillinger to the Day Road place was probably the judge's salvation. The spirits had passed him over.

But Madge was wary nevertheless. Anyone who ventured into the Majerosky driveway was under suspicion and vulnerable. After all, in suspicion and hostility is the crux of this drama. Two centuries ago the native peoples were not suspicious and wary enough. That is why they had disappeared into the spirit world. They had not been cautious enough. Therefore, their land had been stolen and their sacred places desecrated.

Madge watched the car stopping near the side entrance to the house. The judge pulled himself from the driver's seat and walked slowly to the door. After knocking he waited. Madge waited. Would he persist? Or would he give up and leave? When he knocked a second time, Madge decided that he and the judge would need to meet.

He stood upright and headed toward the house. Within seconds, he could see that the Judge had spotted him and began walking toward Madge.

"Mr. Majerosky, hello! My name is Harry Shillinger. I'm almost a neighbor. On the river." He shouted from a distance. "How are you"?

Madge was silent until they stood face to face at arm's length apart. Then he made a grunting noise as a way of letting the judge know he was not deaf. "What can I do for you, Judge?" He spoke in a monotone.

"Just seeing you're up and about is enough," he put on his congenial face, "I'm looking around for information about the terrible things that are happening here these days. I suppose the police have started checking with the neighbors, but I've got my own curiosity. Did you see anything strange the other night when the Kreutzer people were murdered?"

Madge reached behind his back to touch his pruning blade as he pondered his answer. "I saw nothing. I was sleeping, of course!"

Reed described the man with the child behind his shed as dressed in black with a heavy beard and a short stocky body. The judge noted that Majerosky was short. The stockiness may have been the result of the clothing that the man wore. To the judge this man was of average build. This man had a very dark beard. There was enough to make the judge pursue further.

"It's an awful thing! To have it happen right next to your property. Aren't you afraid?"

Madge answered, "Not afraid. Not inclined to be afraid of anything. Besides I'm not the type who gets slaughtered in the night."

The judge commented. "Well, none of us are! But a lot of folks lately have been dying in London Township. The sheriff has called them suicides, but they could have all been cleverly planned murders. That's my suspicion."

Madge jerked his head to the right then to the left as if to shake off an insect, ran his hand over his face, and walked toward the judge. As he did so he stared over the judge's shoulder to make it clear that this conversation was over.

The judge acknowledged, "Well sir. I need to get on my way. Nice meeting you, Mr. Majerosky." And with those words, the judge took several steps toward his car.

Madge wheeled on his heels and in three silent steps was directly behind the judge and reaching around the front of his body. With the other hand he reached behind his own back and deftly removed the pruning knife from his belt. The judge blurted an expletive as his head was wrenched backward in the strong grip that Madge had. But before the rest of the judge's body could react the blade had slid across his throat biting deeply into his flesh and was immediately engulfed in dark red blood pouring from the wound.

The judge's face locked into the shocked expression that had come with the expletive. There was nothing more. The judge's life was drained away in a fraction of a second. He was hardly able to acknowledge what was happening to him. Everything about the judge was over. Especially everything that the man could use to expose his murderer was gone. To Madge that was the important fact.

Madge had not killed the judge for any other reason. This murder was most unpleasant for him. Madge was a priest not a sociopath. This man had to die. There had never been a time previously when he had come this close to disclosure. He was very careful never to talk to others in the community. This was not the result of a character trait. It was part of his plan to fulfill his life's work. He was placed on earth by the Great Spirit to be a mediator between humanity and the spirit world. Some would be transferred to that world through his sacrifices and the others would be redeemed by those sacrifices and the earth would be avenged. Madge was a priest not a murderer. However, he had more work to do. There was the possibility that there was an end in sight, but this judge was a threat to Madge's future. The man had to die.

Madge looked down at the body on the ground in front of him. He had to dispose of it. Other killings, the sacrifices, needed to be witnessed by others. The sacrifices needed to be known even though most people would not know the true meaning of the deaths.

This murder needed to remain a secret for as long as possible. As far as he knew the judge's visit was not witnessed by anyone. But he had to think. His clothes, everything he wore would have to be destroyed. The blood flow had been tremendous. The ground around the body was saturated. And, of course there was the body and the judge's car.

Madge searched the judge's pockets for the keys to the car. Quickly looking around he moved the car to the horse barn nearby. After opening the large sliding door he carefully drove into the barn and closed the door. It was important that no one drive by and see that Madge had a visitor. With that done, Madge could think about what he would do with the body. He wasn't long in coming to a conclusive plan.

He walked hurriedly to the tool shed behind the house. He knew exactly what he would do. In his thoughts the plan was perfect. Every winter just before the first signs of spring when the temperatures hover most of day and every night around the freezing mark, farmers in the area used to butcher hogs. The carcass of every hog simply disappears. Unlike beef, there is no hide to haul away or giant mounds of guts. Everything is used. That thought brought a smile of accomplishment to Madge's normally unsmiling countenance. When he entered the dark shed he found the kettle immediately.

Within a few minutes, the kettle was set, the fire kindled, and he dragged the body of the judge to the kettle. After an hour or so the water began to boil. Madge lifted the body of the judge to the lip of the huge kettle and slipped it inch by inch into the boiling water. He moved several pieces of his best firewood to the vicinity to make sure that the long burning fire would not draw attention to itself with a smoky column for neighbors to see. Then he went about the other business of his day. It could take a couple days, but eventually the carcass of the old judge would be totally decomposed and ready for easy dispersal in non-detectable pieces.

The problem was the car! Madge told himself that patience was the best approach. An inspired solution was surely available. He simply needed to wait.

He could not afford to wait much longer to finish the task of the sacrifice. He could feel the enemies closing in on him. He congratulated himself on his good fortune. Each one of the sacrifices had been completed in plain sight. Each one was disguised in a minimal way. Madge had thought carefully about each action. His work was artistic in that sense. After each sacrifice he added another element of disclosure to the scene. The murder of the Kreutzer people was the best example. For the first time, he made no effort to disguise the fact that the deaths were, in fact, murders. Previous to these acts, he had left the dead in a posture or attitude indicating accidental death or suicide. In the case of the Kreutzers, he had dumped two of the bodies into the well and the other was carefully placed in the opening of a drain tile.

Madge had long resented the defilement of the land and the white man's ability to inevitably disturb the manner in which nature takes care of its own. In this case, the issue was water. Before the white man came, the land was nourished by the presence of ground water. The soil had risen from the ancient swamp but was not entirely dehydrated. Below the surface was a moist and nourishing residue. The People needed water, but they took it from the river. The Great Spirit had gathered water there in the ancient times in order for the People to use it. The river supplied water to drink, to support the planting of corn, and to bathe. It was the Great Spirit's plan. But the white man chose to make his own rivers. He dug ditches, and when a road crossed a ditch, he added a huge tile to allow the water to flow through the road bed. Instead of the white man's women walking to the river for water, they dug wells near their dwellings to collect water for drinking, cooking, and bathing. Therefore, the Kreutzer deaths were his way of redeeming the land from the insults of the white man. With one last sacrifice to complete, Madge waited for the inspiration that would help him send a final message to the enemy.

Chapter Seventeen

In the dim moments near dawn, Reed slipped from Caren's bed and dressed. Many like Reed live hoping they might recover something that reminded them of a youthful ecstasy. Reed's thoughts were not there. Rather he thought of this first feeling; something never before experienced by him. As he slipped from the room and out the front door, he shook his head in disbelief at his luck.

The news came three days later. Judge Shillinger had disappeared. One of his friends, who played euchre with the judge every Friday at the Grange hall in Grape, stopped by the tavern, and then called the sheriff. The judge's car was missing, the dog was locked in the back room of the house, and the neighbors said he would have contacted them before leaving town, even if it were a sudden decision to leave. The police began cruising the country roads and sent one diving crew to the various water holes and lakes around the county. They started with the old quarry at Twin Lakes.

Two deep black holes in the earth - Madge's ancestors had never seen them. The deep holes were the creation of modern entrepreneurs. Twin Lakes was a private set of swimming holes which in a previous existence were stone quarries. The water never moved. Deep in the dark inaccessible origin of these small lakes was a source that kept them filled and cold. There was no light at that depth. So there was no movement, no flutter of fabric, no wave of the boney, dead extremity that hovered in the water above the small, slow current of the artesian pump. There was no glitter from the reflection of light off the mirror of the judge's car that hung like a dive bomber held in suspension a few feet from the ice cream cone-like bottom of the smaller Twin Lake. And when the diving teams from the sheriff's office went below, they circled above the wreckage. Before they entered the deeper darkness where they might have seen the burlap sack containing the judge's remains, they gave up the search because of rusting debris and the cold.

Chapter Eighteen

After disposing of the judge's remains and the vehicle, Madge began to experience a new feeling. Never before had he been anxious about the discretion taken by him to cover his identity and connection with the killings. Perhaps it was his uncanny ability to understand the thought processes of the whites. Therefore, he instinctively took steps to guard against any possibility that the authorities might capture him before he could complete his mission. He knew that the disappearance of the well-known respected judge of the county would make these whites double their efforts to solve the mystery. Unlike the People, the whites valued the famous and the powerful more than those whose lives were more mundane and closer to the earth.

It takes ten minutes to travel from the Twin Lakes to the Majerosky farm; that is, if you travel by automobile. Madge never owned an automobile. Every where he went he walked. Usually walking the roads was comfortable for him, but today was different, and Madge was determined that until he finished his task he would be invisible. The ancient "wendigo" was never seen, but its work was always shockingly visible. Madge would do the impossible. He would kill the last interloper and not one person, except one, would know the perpetrator. So Madge did not leave by the gate of the Twin Lakes enclosure that day. After climbing the chain link fence surrounding the area he set off through the woods and hidden fields, heading directly for the river. Several times he had to cross roads that were seldom traveled. He was always careful to walk in the open only when he knew that human dwellings were far enough away that he would not be seen. It took him three hours to make the journey back to his farm. It was several hours until dawn when he arrived.

He entered the house and walked directly to his medicine cabinet. A single light over the mirror illuminated the small space of his bathroom and the dark visage of his own face. He began with the scissors and hacked away at the dense scruff of his beard and hair. When there was nothing left but a shadowy covering he began to shave. An hour later Madge saw what had never been visible to him or any other human being for 30 years. While his body was husky, wide, and muscular, his face had become craggy, twisted with a permanent frown and his eyes hidden in dark sockets under a broad and wrinkled forehead.

He gathered tools, extra blankets, several knives, and several bags of flour and wrapped them in a wool blanket that covered his bed. Just before dawn as the light of day barely showed in the east, Madge left his house for the last time. He walked to the edge of the woods west of his house, dropped the pack and returned to the barn. He spent the next fifteen minutes emptying every gasoline container that he could find over various points at the foundations of all the buildings including the house. He left one container with a small amount of gasoline in each against the inside wall near the doors of each building. The final step was to soak five-foot lengths of rope in the gasoline and insert them into each can. Before entering the woods Madge struck a match to each rope.

He was at least a mile into the wooded strip at the back of his farm when he glanced back to see that a large black cloud of smoke was billowing into the sky. Twenty minutes after that he heard the distant whine of the fire engines from Maybee. He smiled to himself. In the twenty minutes that the fire burned undetected, any evidence that the Majerosky family ever lived would be covered with hot ashes. Madge walked south until he came to the edge of the wooded area that bordered on the fields of the Kreutzer farm. Then just as the morning was beginning to warm, he dropped the pack against a large tree, removed a blanket, and with the pack as a pillow he fell into a deep sleep.

Madge dreamed. A pale young man stepped from behind a great hickory a few feet to his right. He was dressed in the leather clothes of a forest dweller. The boy walked to Madge's feet and dropped to knees and stared into Madge's peaceful face. He waited. In his subconscious Madge heard a voice calling for him to awake, "Take my hand, New Father. Lead me to a new future. Show me where you have been." Madge shook his head until he opened his eyes and saw nothing there. The boy had vanished. The day was nearly gone but not wasted. He knew that there was a new day for him and his people. As the darkness fell Madge crossed the Kreutzer fields to the deserted farm buildings across from Shillinger's place. Entering the barn, he climbed to the loft and sat at the small opening in the peak of the gable. From there he watched as Reed's tan pick-up pulled into the driveway and stopped at the house. "I'll wait," he said, "I'll wait for the time when you will be ready to do what I ask you to do,"

Chapter Nineteen

Reed returned from an afternoon of stunning developments. A monster fire had destroyed every building on the Majerosky farm across the way. He learned of the fire from a deputy that he met while making a stop at the judge's house. As he approached and turned into the lane he was shocked by the flashing lights of a sheriff's cruiser sitting near the entrance to the house. The deputy was standing at the open door of the cruiser talking into his communication unit. As Reed approached, he hooked it into its place in the cruiser and turned to Reed.

"Can I help you, sir?" he quizzed.

"I'm here to visit the judge. Is something wrong?

"We don't know for sure. Do you have business with the judge?

Reed stopped near the rear of the cruiser.

"Not really. Just a visit. I'm Reed Shillinger, one of the Judge's anonymous relatives. I hadn't seen him for a couple weeks so I decided to check in."

The deputy decided to probe, "The judge isn't here. No one has seen him for several days. I don't know you, but your name is familiar. Have we met?"

Reed remembered. "We met before. The night that the Kreutzer family was murdered. I'm living in the farmhouse across the way on Day Road. In fact, the last time I talked to the judge we talked about that."

"Listen Mr. Shillinger, there are some strange things going on around here. The judge's car is gone. His neighbors haven't seen him or his car for several days. Last night the Majerosky place went up in flames, and old Madge has disappeared as well. Did the judge say anything that would connect him with old Madge?"

"I can't be sure. The judge was very informed about a lot of strange deaths in the area over the last few years. We talked about the Kreutzer deaths and he hinted that there might be connections."

Another deputy came out of the back door of the judge's house and called to them, "You better get in here Nathan. There's something you oughta see."

Nathan turned to Reed. "Do you know the judge very well?"

Reed nodded tentatively.

"Then come along"

The two of them walked into the house and the two deputies and Reed hovered over a cluttered stack of old papers on the table in the house. There were maps, old ones, and documents that looked like land descriptions and deeds.

"Nathan, here's what's interesting. There is an abstract of sorts here about the land that the judge owns. The maps are a little tough to decipher, but I think that they show the land the judge owns, the Kreutzer farm and the place where a Shillinger family lived back in the 50s. But, if you look real carefully, there's a handwritten note on the map in between the judge's land and the Shillinger's. It is hard to read but I'd bet a week's pay that word is "Majerosky."

"Isn't that the place that burned down this morning? And Majerosky is nowhere to be found?" he asked.

"Right! Funny coincidence don't you think?" the two deputies talked as if Reed wasn't there.

Reed and the deputy studied the document. There was no doubt. The farm where Reed was living, the judge's place, the Kreutzer place, and the Majerosky place had once been the same parcel of land during the time when the French took it from the Native Americans.

"If this was the last thing that the judge was looking at before he left the house, I'm thinking we ought to look for a trace of him at the Majerosky place."

In the deep blackness of the Twin Lakes near its artesian source a bubble caught the undercarriage of the judge's car. No living ear heard the scraping as the car tilted forward and over. To the world above the only visible sign of movement was a tiny ripple and nothing more. The bag with its gruesome contents drifted deeper and deeper. The deputies' search through the burned out remains of the Majerosky buildings revealed nothing. The judge and his life slipped into the dimming memory of the land and the neighbors.

Chapter Twenty

Over the winter, Reed took a job at the SuperRite grocery store managed by the family that once owned it but had since sold out to the larger chain. They took Reed on to cover the vacations of those employees who escaped each year to the warmth of Florida. One week he worked in the warehouse, another as a clerk, and eventually they kept him on as a stocker. It was on the way home from work that Reed had stopped at the judge's house. He had promised to have supper with Sam and Daisy that evening. A few minutes to change clothes and he was on his way. In the darkness, his new neighbor from the haymow of the Kreutzer barn came to call.

Later that evening Sam and Daisy sat with their son in the living room. The television was on as the three of them searched their minds for a topic of conversation. When the local news announced the breaking story of the disappearance of Judge Shillinger and the speculations about connections with a man named Majerosky who also had disappeared the same day that his farmhouse and buildings had all burned to the ground, Reed asked Sam about the Day Road place.

"I was over to visit Harry this afternoon when the deputies were there. They showed me some strange documents that mentioned our place on Day Road. What happened when we left the place?" Reed asked.

"Well, I don't know much about that stuff. Harry owned it and your grand-dad rented it until we took over and rented too." Sam was very abrupt.

"Why did we leave?"

"Ol' Harry decided to sell it, that's why. And I didn't want to be paying rent to some stranger is about the sum total of it."

"You mean we never owned it? These old documents said that at one time Jacob and Peter Shillinger owned a large parcel of land that stretched from the river all the way back to near Stone Road. Wasn't Jacob your grandfather?"

"Yeah. That's true. But Jacob had so many kids that when he died his half had to be divided. Your grandpa got only a small part of it. And you know Reed; your grandpa was not a very wise farmer. Eventually, he got Harry who was a part of Peter Shillinger's family to buy it and let him stay on, work the farm, and pay rent."

It was obvious that Sam didn't think much of the story of that farm and its connection to the Shillinger family. So he tried to steer that conversation into a different direction.

"What do you know about this guy named Majerosky?"

Sam rubbed his whole face with his hand the way he always did when he wanted a conversation to end.

"All I know is what little you can know about a distant neighbor and a little more from what dad always told us about the family. You know most of us thought he was a little crazy. He would wander the roads back there and bother people for handouts and stuff. That wasn't always. Sometimes he'd just walk around the places nearby, kinda snoopin' and such. Didn't talk much but he could waste a lot of your time. Most of the women around were a little afraid of him. You might remember the time he came over here when I was in town to get feed for the cows?"

"I remember that. Is he the guy with the big knife?"

"That's the one. It was a vintner's knife. Never could figure why he couldn't leave that thing at home! And dad used to tell us that he was not total Polish. His parents actually bought that piece of land back when dad was living there and your aunt and I were teenagers?

"What do you mean he wasn't total Polish?"

"Well, Dad said that he was part Indian. His mother was a full-blooded Indian. They came over from Canada and bought that farm from the people who had bought from my aunt, your grandpa's sister."

"I hope that its coincidence – the fact that since I have been here five people have been killed and everyone has been living on land that was once one piece. Come to think of it, that one parcel was owned by our family. I sure wouldn't want to be the object of some strange vendetta."

"Sure is coincidence, son. You can always move back to Texas and be with your family. There aren't any Shillinger skeletons there. Unless you've started some on your own."

"Could be. I certainly have a knack for letting my life get out of hand these days. Speaking of Texas, dad, I'll tell you one thing that I miss. It's the sun. I had forgotten how seldom you see it around here. Even when you get a break in the clouds it doesn't last very long."

The phone in the kitchen rang and Daisy went to answer it. The conversation stopped long enough for Reed to hear Daisy say Evelyn's name. Immediately, Reed walked to the kitchen and took the phone from his mother's hand.

"What's happening, Evie? It's been a while."

"It's about Jack, Reed."

"What about him. Is he alright?"

"I suppose you'd say he is. But he is acting real strange lately. In the last month he has taken up with a bad crowd at school, his grades have fallen off, and yesterday I found a package of marijuana in his backpack."

"That's more than strange, Evie. What's going on? He's only eleven."

"Reed, don't start down the road I think you are. You haven't exactly been a steady role model for him. Here's what I'm thinking. Suppose you take him for a while? Can you do that?"

"It's possible. I don't exactly have a great place for him. Find out if he is willing to come here. Then if he seems comfortable send him over Christmas break. That will give me time to get him settled here and in a school."

"Thanks, Reed. It tears me apart but maybe it will help and we'll be able to figure out what we're going to do with the rest of our lives."

"I know, Evie. I really messed things up for all of us. Tell Jennifer I love her."

It didn't take long after Reed put the phone down for Daisy to start on her plan for Jack's coming. The Day Road place was not a proper place for a boy, and she and Sam would be happy to have both of them live here. Reed started for the door saying something about needing to think about it and how he would be in touch. By the time he was on the road, he felt the desperation return.

Very soon Reed decided what to do first. He headed for Monroe to talk to Caren. She would help him make the right arrangements. He laughed out loud at himself when he acknowledged how helpless he was as a parent. He talked to his son so seldom and in sentences and conversations so short, he could remember few of them. Every choice that was made for the children had been made in a consultative process. The process was Evie decides, Reed listens to Evie, and the children became recipients of Evie's wise choices. Honestly, the decisions were very wise more often than not. What tied Reed into knots was the fact that he never really listened to her so the wisdom was lost in the moment.

Caren was immediately aware that something had happened. She saw the stiffness around Reed's mouth and the eyes that constantly moved up to the right and never focused on her face. She observed that the greeting at the door was rushed and perfunctory.

"Jack's coming to stay with me, Caren. I don't know what to do," he finally said after many attempts to set up the conversation so that he could dodge as many tough questions as possible, Caren listened and interrupted, "Let's go. We're going out to the farm. We'll take the girls in my car and we'll try to come up with a plan. You can do this, Reed. I know you can."

Chapter Twenty One

Madge waited until darkness made it impossible to see across the way to the farmhouse where Reed lived. He left the Kreutzer barn and walked the lane toward the road. As he entered the driveway to Reed's place he stopped to make sure he saw no approaching cars. He made a circuit around the house and tested all the doors and windows. All were locked or frozen from age and decay. When he tested a couple of bulkhead doors that led into the cellar, he discovered that the latch was a simple loop with a piece of wood in it. Madge had found the perfect entrance. Once inside he closed the door without a sound and descended the short set of steps. The cellar was absolutely without light.

But Madge waited until his eyes were adjusting to the darkness before he moved forward. Soon it was possible for him to see most shapes and avoid bumping into rafters and support beams. An old coal furnace filled one of the small rooms but it was not working. This was good. He wouldn't have to worry about the inhabitant coming to the cellar to keep the house warm. Silently, Madge inspected every room.

Next he needed to find a way to the upper floors of the house. He found the stairs leading to the first floor and carefully tested them. He ascended and tested the door. It made a rusty sound as he opened it. With the door open a crack he stopped and listened. The house was still empty. Madge entered a small back room off the kitchen. There was more light at this level so Madge moved quickly inspecting each room. Occasionally he would become like a statue and listen intently to make sure no one was in the house or about to enter it. He sat down on the couch in the nearly vacant living room where he had seen the Shillinger man and his woman making love. His hands gently caressed the couch surface as he sat remembering everything he learned about the man. He decided that the woman could live. She had nothing to do with Madge's plan to take vengeance.

Then he went to the stairway leading to the upper story. He noted that one or two of the steps groaned when his weight settled down on them. If he were to attack the man while he was upstairs, he would have to ascend with speed before the man could respond to the creaking sounds from the stairway. He walked into the room where Reed slept. Near the bed was a large tank holding water. Perfect! He would take the man in his sleep and do it next to water. He sat on the bed, and, again, his hands moved slowly over the surface. He reached over to a stack of clothes and took a shirt. He stuffed it into his pocket, left the room, and made his way back to the cellar door. The sound of a car engine and slamming of car doors brought him to a standstill. For a second he thought about confronting him then, but decided to hide in the cellar. Deftly he descended the steps and squatted behind the old furnace.

He listened as the group came into the house. The woman must have come with the man, and he heard the lighter and quicker footsteps of children. Madge remained completely still and listened for any signs that they might be entering the cellar. He could hear bits of their conversation.

"You'll probably have to move from that awful room with the water tank. Jack will feel better if you are near him on this floor. After all, there are plenty of rooms down here." The woman said.

"You're right. But what about furniture and a kitchen where I can do some cooking. I'm pretty sloppy about that. Jack needs real meals." Madge heard Reed's voice for the first time.

"Reed, I have a lot of furniture stored when I downsized after the divorce. We'll find everything you need. I think there is another bed in that locker.

"I'm sure that it will work, Caren. Sure couldn't do this without your help. If Jack were not eleven but older, it might be a different story. At least this way I can tell my mother and father that I can handle it. I guess he might have to stay with his grandparents when he's not in school and I'm working."

Madge could hardly contain his excitement. As the voices came through the old heating ducts it was as if a messenger brought the exact information that he needed to complete his task. The Shillinger man was bringing his son into the house. His exuberance was barely containable. Madge cautiously moved to the cellar door and made his exit. As he slipped through the door on to the ground he rolled on his back to make sure he had not been seen. Suddenly he saw two yellow green eyes staring at him from the limb of a large walnut tree twenty feet away and twenty feet up. He remembered the dream of the boy who called him "New Father." The window above the bulkhead doors sent light into the eyes of the huge bird in the tree. But Madge knew that those eyes were meant for him. As he slithered away into the shadows far enough away that it was safe to stand, Madge heard again the sound of wings beating the air above him and going into the distance. There was no moon that night so Madge's walk down the lane to the Kreutzer barn was a dance. It was the dance of a man who knew his great moment had come. The plan was in place to avenge the destruction of the great Fire People and, in the capture of a son, to extend the life of their presence here. He would be the one to fulfill it.

Chapter Twenty Two

The winter in Monroe County harassed it residents through the months from December to March. Frozen layers of ice and snow encased the countryside. December greeted young Jack from Texas with intense cold but no snow. The two January thaws lasted 24 hours each and were followed by rain that turned to a fluffy snow. Of all the good things about winter in Michigan, snow has to be at the top of the list. When Jack arrived the ground was hard, frozen into the shapes left with the rains and the muddy rutting of November. The Shillingers, grandparents and parent, worked tirelessly to make the move as painless as possible.

Reed worked odd schedules at the super market, but Sam and Daisy were always available to cover. It was the time at the farm when Reed and Jack were alone that most challenged Reed. The place had reshaped this grown-up into a doubtful, hesitant, and almost adolescent caught in a grown man's body. The hidden places in the barns, the wooded lots, and the shallow creek passing through the stockyards behind the barns were too familiar to Reed for him to appreciate the sense of adventure that overtook his son every day. Until the first days of January, Jack was at the farm or at the grandparents every day. The Christmas holiday was full of excitement as always, but the farm was a setting made for an eleven year old boy.

The situation for Madge was completely different. His home was now the loft in the Kreutzer barn. Since he had moved in there after the burning of his own place every minute of daylight was spent there. He could never be seen and no evidence that he was alive would ever come to light. Madge switched his night and day schedule, sleeping from dawn to dusk and eating, working, planning, and stalking the object of his work at night.

On a day between Christmas and the New Year, Reed was scheduled to be at work at seven in the evening. He had slept the day away and awoke at four in the afternoon. The thought that Jack might not be in another room or just a shout away never occurred to him. Reed and Jack had agreed that no matter what Jack might be doing, he would need to check in before darkness fell. That particular night the sky was especially heavy with clouds. It looked as if a storm, either snow or rain, might be approaching. In which case, darkness came sooner and more suddenly. Reed stepped out to the side porch and called Jack's name. To his relief he heard an answer from the horse barns across the farmyard from where Reed stood. As soon as he heard Jack's voice, the boy himself burst through the door of the barn and waved. Reed felt that strange tingle that fathers feel when they notice for the first time that the son who seemed such a stranger was actually a smaller version of himself.

"I'm OK, dad. Can I stay out just a little longer? I'll be in this barn."

Reed said he would call him in twenty minutes for supper and went back into the house.

Jack ran into the barn and back on the ladder to the loft above the horse stalls. He was on an imaginary treasure hunt. Since the day after Christmas while exploring the many buildings Jack had come across wonderful toys. They looked like toy creatures. One day as he rambled his way into the rickety building formerly known as the chicken coop, something hanging from above his head slammed into his eye. It hurt so bad it took him a minute to be curious enough to find out what hit him. He looked up and saw a carved wooden figure of a bear. It was attached to a flimsy string hanging from the rafters. It was small enough to stick into his pocket. He never thought about telling his dad. In a place like this farm, where everything is strange, nothing is actually worthy of comment.

The man in the shadows hiding behind the stacks of chicken crates in the far corner was grateful. From the first time he saw Jack he knew this was the one who would become his son. The carved figures were the first installments in the re-education process of this beautiful boy. It was the Great Spirit's will that Jack Shillinger become Shabonee, the child of Nashiwaskuk of the Bird Clan of the Fire People. Every day Madge placed a figurine in one of the outbuildings of the Shillinger farm. The boy had found the bear, the wolf, and the buffalo. He had yet to find the bird which perched precariously on the top rung of the ladder to the loft in the horse barn.

Madge knew that this was the night when Jack would discover the last gift. Madge was hiding in the far recesses of the hayloft surrounded by old, dusty, and broken down bales of hay. He stared at the ladder, the only way in or out of the loft. He could hear the scuffling and imaginary conversations of the boy as he played below. There was a moment of quiet just before he saw the top of the ladder shudder. The boy was coming up. Madge prepared the tape for the boy's mouth and the rope which would be used to tie his hands and his feet. He moved closer to the edge of the loft ready to spring the trap as soon as the boy stepped from the ladder and on the floor of the loft. At his first glimpse of the top of Jack's head, he heard the voice of boy's father calling from the house. Immediately the boy stopped, changed hands on the top rung, and turned to listen. When he moved his hand he knocked the figurine from its perch. Later, after Jack had permission to stay a little longer, he ran back into the barn to find what he had knocked from the ladder. First, he mounted the ladder, then hesitated trying to remember where he had seen the figurine last. Hanging there he looked down and saw it lying in the straw and dust on the floor of the barn. Jack never returned to the loft that day and Madge's trap was never tripped.

Jack burst into the kitchen with the wooden carving in his hand.

"Dad, look what I found in the barn. It's a carving of a bird."

"Let me see. That looks freshly carved. You found it in the horse barn today?"

"Yup! Isn't it great? I'm going to put in my box with the others. I have a collection of them. Found them all out there." His enthusiasm was on overload.

"But Jack, these are practically new. When we have time I'd like to see them"

During their meal Reed could think of little else. How could freshly carved figurines end up in those barns without someone putting them there? If such were the case, Reed couldn't think of anything good happening with an unknown carver of wooden figurines wandering around in the farm buildings where Jack loved to play. He looked at the clock. It was time to get Jack over to his grandparents to spend the night while he was at work.

When he arrived at Sam and Daisy's, Sam was waiting for him at the door. He asked Reed for permission to take Jack ice fishing the next day. They would go to the lake in the afternoon and probably would not return until late in the evening so it would be better for Jack to stay an extra night. Reed checked with Jack, and he was excited about it. It meant that Reed would have a rare opportunity to meet Caren for supper the next evening.

Reed left work that day with thoughts about his future. He had returned to Michigan because the past had devoured his future. For the first few months the past was sorted into categories of comfortable and painful. Mostly painful since the jarring reminders in the landscape and the sky, the people and the way they lived were on his doorstep instead of a thousand miles distant. His mind directed his heart to live only in the comfortable. His relationship with Caren began in that cozy pigeonhole of remembered feelings, childish urges, and terminal happenstance. He thought about the way memories good and bad can be smothered in new experience; especially when the intruder is a complete and giving person like Caren. She came to him at the riverside in her present, and over the last few months had enticed him ever so gently to the place where he, too, was living in the present. Any brightness or lightness around him was a gift from her.

If there was any cloud on Reed's horizon, it crept over him from the hidden part of his interior dome. Guilt drifted over him in the blurry overcast of his personal regrets: the early years of rejecting the awkwardly offered love from his parents, his secret desires covered up by his misshapen code of the acceptable and unacceptable, and the years with Evelyn when he recited lines and followed stage directions written by an author who demanded an actor not a whole person.

Anxiety surged inside as he approached Caren's house. The Pretender was ready to act again. Impulsively he hit the brakes and pulled to a curb. Reed grabbed his head and leaned on the steering wheel. His face was contorted and twisted from an agony of spirit. As often happened, Reed spoke words that sounded prayerful without even a hint that he believed that there was One who might hear it. Sighing deeply the prayer came out, "Show me how to belong to my present and my past; to Caren, Jack, Jennifer, Evie, Sam and Daisy." He leaned back, took a deep breath, and drove away.

Caren opened the door. She was dressed in a red sweater and jeans. Her face was clean and her hair softly reflecting the remaining afternoon light. Her smile invited him to come to her, and he did. He embraced and held on with a kind of desperation. She could feel the turbulence of his spirit, and she received it.

"Can you come with me to the farm?"

Gently pulling away she said, "Mom and Dad are coming to take the children to exchange some Christmas gifts. Let's have supper and when they leave, I can go with you."

Later, while in the car, Reed talked incessantly. It was a hurried tour in which he was showing Caren his private place for the first time; so he talked about his past on the farm, the house and the few years that he lived there.

"You need to know that this house is the only place where I have ever felt safe, Caren. I was seven when we left. My memories of Sam and Daisy from the Day Road place are a universe away from memories of those same people in the other place. I was protected there. Mom kept me close to her every day. Dad took my hand and showed me the world from here. After we moved I was always fighting to find mom, and dad was too busy to show me anything except the cramped world of his work and smothering needs of the new place."

They sat on the old couch in the nearly empty living room. Reed hesitated, searching for a response from her. She moved closer and touched his knee.

"With Jack here, I am trying to make it all fit together; you, me and my children."

"It's going to take time, Reed. I know that. Both of us need to take a deep breath. I began to fit you into my life with the children that first day at the river. I've had a lot of practice over the last few months."

"Then I hope you can wait for me. It is as if we have been together at a distance; speed travel until a few months ago, but now the slow plodding at the end of a mapped road. Since Jack came I am more aware of life's complications, but, at least I'm back to living again."

"You still are not at ease with this place. Do you know why?"

"It's like a cloud is hanging over my head – that's what it is. I can't figure it out. Just last night dad was talking about his take on the disappearance of Judge Harry, a relative of ours."

"I knew that, but how does that make you uneasy?"

"It's probably my morbid imagination, but the fact is that Judge Harry, the Kreutzer family and I all live on the same old land parcel. It was a French claim in the 1700's that my great grandfather and great uncle bought in the 1840's. Dad just dismissed it as my personal fancy, but I still feel threatened in a way. An example is Jack's playful exploring of the farm."

"Certainly you're not afraid that he'll get hurt? You know where he is most of the time don't you?"

"Even so, Caren, last night before supper he came in with a small carving of a bird that he had found in the horse barn. Didn't get my attention until he told me that he had found three others like it since he's been here. This carving was a new one – not like some long lost antique toy. I can't help wonder how these toys happened to end up in these barns."

"You're thinking that someone is hiding them? Leaving them for Jack to find? That is a little scary."

"Right! I'll have to watch Jack more closely when he's outside. I hope that will give me more peace of mind."

Caren moved closer and put her arms around Reed.

"I will help as much as I can, Reed. But right now let's help each other." She smiled and kept going. "I know how to make you feel safe right here."

As the two of them snuggled close, they were startled by a scraping sound coming from below. Startled, Reed stood and listened.

"Christ! What was that?"

Caren tried to pull him back to the couch. "Probably some wild animal has found a way to keep warm in your cellar."

Reed relaxed. Safe was only a small part of what he wanted to feel right then, so he joined Caren and she loved him.

Chapter Twenty Three

That night, Madge carefully made his way to the Shillinger place. He carried with him a clothe sack with rope and wide packing tape. Again, he was prepared to take the final steps of his plan to rid the land of Reed Shillinger and capture a son to carry on his name. His plan to take the boy in the loft had failed, but Madge was a patient man. Having failed in the first attempt he actually believed that this new idea was better. Since yesterday he had noticed that neither the boy nor the father had been at the house the whole day. Later he saw the man return with his woman, but the boy was not with them. It would be a long wait. If necessary he would hide in the cellar that night and into the next day.

Madge was counting on the snow holding off for at least one more day. After he captured the boy he would need to leave the Kreutzer place to witness the final sacrifice. He was sure that the police and sheriff would soon close in and find his hiding place. He circled the buildings as he did the first time, and he entered the cellar by the bulkhead doors. The doors opened as easily as before, but this time as he was closing them the hinges scraped and made an audible groan. Madge dropped to a squat so that the door could come completely closed and waited. The man and woman were somewhere in the house and the sound was loud enough that surely they had heard it. Madge waited in that position for a quarter hour or so. When he was sure that it was safe to move he stepped into the cellar, squatted near the furnace, and listened. He heard human sounds above, but the conversation was so low that he could not understand what they were saying. Several hours later and Madge had heard no sounds, especially the sound of the boy. He settled down to wait for the morning or even longer. Halfway through the night he heard the man and the woman moving around from one room to another. From his memory of the floor plan he guessed that they had started in the living room then went to a room on the second floor, probably the one next to the tank room. They were sleeping together. Madge added another detail to his plan. The boy would be sleeping in the first floor bedroom and the man would be on the second floor. If this turned out to be true the likelihood of interference from the man when Madge attempted to take the boy was minimized.

As morning approached, Madge heard more sounds from above. It would be more than convenient if both the man and woman were to leave the house. One hour would give him time to walk through and finalize the plan. An hour after sunup they left the house and Madge heard the sound of an automobile fading toward the road and off the property.

The house was empty. Madge again ascended the stairs to the first floor. He searched through the pantry. He found two important items; a loaf of bread from which took two pieces and ate, and a can of Three-in One oil. From the pantry he went to the bedroom where the boy would likely be sleeping. He was content to see that he had been right. As he searched through the drawers of the night stand he found the carvings he had left for the boy. He noted that there was no door on the room and went upstairs to find the man's bedroom. He took a minute or two to acknowledge his respect for a man who moved from the rough cot next to the water tank into a bedroom furnished in a more traditional way. As he descended the stairs, he identified the two stair treads that squeaked when he stepped on them. Three times he went up and down and then up again. Each time the same two steps made the noise. The fourth time he went down and skipped the two noisy ones. One more time he walked back up. Again he skipped the two that might give his approach away. The last trip up was absolutely silent. He inspected Reed's bed carefully and determined from the way the mattress was worn what part of the bed Reed normally occupied. Madge took a deep breath and looked around. He was satisfied that he had done everything that could be done to prepare. Without looking back he left the second floor. He stopped at the door at the bottom of the stairs and put a small drop of oil on each hinge, moved the door back and forth until it made no sound opening or closing. It did the same to the door going to the cellar, then turned, took the two slices of bread from the kitchen table, and re-entered the cellar. After removing the large vintner's knife from the belt on his back, he curled up next to the old furnace, slowly ate the bread, and immediately fell asleep.

Madge was awakened from a refreshing sleep by the sounds of footsteps on the floor above. He could hear the voices of a man and a boy. He smiled at his good fortune. The boy had been away temporarily. Madge admitted to himself that there were moments when he feared the boy had been sent away. The next step in the preparation was for Madge to go through the steps in his mind; the capturing of the boy and the conversation he would have with the doomed father.

Upstairs Reed followed his son through the kitchen and into the boy's bedroom. "Dad, remember you said you wanted to see the toy animals that I found? Come here."

Jack opened the drawer and handed the figures to Reed. The carving was rough, but there was no question as to what they were supposed to represent. The buffalo, the bear, the wolf, and the bird.

"What kind of a bird do you think this is, Jack? Looks like an owl, right?"

"Right, dad. That's an owl. That's a bear. A wolf. A buffalo." Jack was sounding like a student reciting his lessons to his teacher.

Reed remembered something about a carved owl. A momentary shiver caught him by surprise. He had heard a story that Coil told him several months ago – on his first day back in Maybee. Before he killed himself, the old barber was seen burying a carved wooden owl along with his barber tools. Reed shrugged away the thought and helped Jack get ready for bed. He left Jack sleeping soundly and went into the kitchen. As he passed the kitchen table he brushed a few crumbs of bread to the floor and reminded himself to say something to Jack the next day about how crumbs lying around bring mice especially in the winter. Not long after that Reed was in his bed. He remembered the bird again, but he was too tired to dwell on it. He turned to his side and fell asleep.

Madge waited for the silence. Difficult as it was he waited until he could wait no more. He found the rope, the tape, and his knife. Slowly he stood and stretched to rid his body of the stiffness. He had worn his moccasins to insure that his footsteps would be silent; step by careful step he deliberately counted each riser of the stairs to the kitchen. Silently he slipped through the door and walked to the boy's room. Even in the darkness he could see the shadow of the boy on the bed. In the room the only sound was the boy's breathing.

Madge walked to the bed. He had placed the roll of tape in his mouth with a short strip unrolled. Reaching over the boy's head, he cupped his hand and pulled toward his body, clamping down on the mouth and nose of Jack, and the boy began a violent struggle, but he was caught, held firmly against Madge's chest. His feet and arms began to flail, but his captor methodically twisted the arms behind the boy's body and with one motion applied the short strip of tape over his mouth.

Holding Jack's arms with one arm, he wrapped a length of rope around them and stretched the rope to the kicking legs and wrapped the ankles in a tight knot. He could not see the terror in the boy's eyes as he laid his own body on Jack until he tired and settled, quiet, bound, and gagged on the bed.

Madge stepped away from the bed and waited until he could breathe normally and rested. Subduing Reed would require strength and quickness so he waited for his muscles and breathing to calm.

Fearing that the boy might begin to bounce and create such a turmoil that Reed could hear, Madge moved hurriedly to the stairs, mounted and counted them as he ascended. Reaching the top of the stairs he removed the knife from his belt and gripped it by the blade. With the stealth of an attacking animal he moved to Reed's bedside, took aim, and swung the handle down over his shoulder and hit Reed sharply on the head. There was a moan and then total silence. Quickly Madge took the rest of the rope and bound Reed hand and foot and rolled him over on his back. Madge sat down on the floor and waited.

A few minutes passed and Reed, regaining consciousness, began to moan. Madge went to the door and turned on the overhead light, grabbed a chair, and sat down near the head of the bed. He stared into Reed's eyes.

"Mr. Shillinger," he sneered out the name, "I have your son tied and gagged downstairs. I assure you he is not hurt, but he is, in fact, in my power."

Reed began to thrash and screamed, "Who are you and what do you want? You won't get away with this." Then Reed stopped speaking and saw Madge's face.

"Yes, we meet again, Mr. Shillinger. I have instructions for you. If you follow them carefully, your son will live a long and valuable life. If you don't do exactly as I tell you, he will die like that little girl you saw me carrying through your farm last fall. Do you understand? You must do everything I say."

"I understand. What do you want from me?"

"Very good." Madge smiled for the first time. "I want you dead. Get it? Dead! Dead by your own hand."

The terror that was mounting inside showed on Reed's face.

"Anything less from you will mean the immediate slaughter of the boy. This is no whim on my part. You are the last of the land stealers. My People demand that you die. They also demand that there be another who knows our story and will carry it to the next generation. Your son will live to tell that story only if you are dead. If you are still alive at sundown the day after tomorrow your son will lie on the earth emptying his life's blood on the land that rightfully belongs to the People, my people."

Reed's body sank into the bedclothes and his eyes began to stare at the ceiling overcome by the realization that the moment had arrived for him to choose; to choose either himself or another. The other was his own son, Jack.

He turned to Madge. "Tell me. What must I do?"

"Listen carefully to these instructions. Next to the burned rubbish that used to be my home, there is an open field and on the other side of it, a hickory break. Day after tomorrow when the sun is highest in the southern sky, around noon as you white people call it, you will drive into that field and in view of the great hickory trees you will kill yourself. Take a moment to register what I am saying. You will kill yourself. You shouldn't grieve too much. Your death will pay the enormous debt owed by generations of your people to generations of my people. And you will save the life of your son. It is very simple; noon, the day after tomorrow in the field next to the hickory trees, on the same land your family stole from mine, you will pay the debt and save your son. I will witness this sacrifice, and you will see your living son there. You will know that because of your last rational act, he is alive and he will not die. Finally, if you call the police or tell anyone what you are about to do, I will know, and your son will die. Do you understand?" Madge paused and gripped Reed's upper arm, "You will trade with me. Your life for the boy."

"I understand." Reed turned again to stare at the ceiling above.

A deep sigh escaped him. When he turned to find him, Madge was gone. He heard his son's voice screaming through the gag. There was the sound of scuffling and footsteps, the closing of a door, and silence.

Reed laid there until noon the next day. He was able to roll to floor, to the stairs, and from there he slid to the first floor. There he finally gave in to the futility. There was no visitor or helper for him. The telephone rang several times during the morning hours. He was sure that it was Caren trying to reach him, but the telephone was mounted on the wall, out of his reach.

All morning long Caren was uneasy. She was also puzzled. This was the day that Reed was going to take Jack to the school to enroll him for the last half of the school year. That appointment was in the afternoon. At last, sensing that something was wrong she gathered the children and drove out to Day Road. Once she was in the driveway, she was sure of her intuition. Reed's car was there, and, leaving her car, she noticed that the door to the kitchen was wide open. She went back to the car and told the children to wait for her in the car. Returning to the house she found Reed, bruised and helpless on the floor of the dining room.

"Caren, thank God you came. I've been lying here since midnight. That mad man, Majerosky, took Jack. I've got something I have to do."

"You're going to call the sheriff. That's what you're doing. Then we're taking you to the emergency room. Here, let me untie those ropes."

"No! Don't call anybody! You need to hear what this is about. Then you have to do nothing."

"Reed, he's kidnapped Jack. The sheriff needs to know. They'll find him."

"Caren, listen, then you'll understand. I have to kill myself and he has to see me do it"

Caren gasped!

"I know. It's macabre, but if I want Jack to live, Majerosky has to see me do it. By noon tomorrow Majerosky needs to see me blow my brains out – in a field on his farm. The deadline is noon, and Jack will be with him the whole time. He'll be watching the clock, and he is fully prepared to slit Jack's throat. If he sees me do it, he will let Jack live. Jack will spend the rest of his days as a slave to him."

"Reed, this is insane! You can't do it! There has to be another way."

"There may be another way, but I haven't thought of it yet. And you can be sure I've had plenty of time to think. You go home with your kids. I need to do this myself, Caren. I'll call you in the morning."

"Reed, am I going to lose you? I can't let you do this."

"You have to leave me alone for now. I promise you, I will call you in the morning when I have decided what to do. I love you, Caren. And I love Jack and Jennifer. That's all that I know for sure now."

Reed held Caren tightly. He kissed her and pushed her away toward the door.

Caren wept as she reluctantly stepped toward the door. Once she was on the porch she ran and was gone in seconds. Reed watched her go, and, like a man in a trance, he walked back into the dining room.

Chapter Twenty Four

In the shadows of the old living room Reed squatted in silence. He had been in that position for nearly 18 hours since sending Caren away. The terror of his encounter with Madge the day before twisted and punched inside the confining flesh of his chest and abdomen. The muscles around his shoulders shook. His eyelids pressed – lid against lid. For an eternity he waited for the terror to go away. Images of past heroics interrupted his fear but gave no comfort or encouragement.

"You will trade with me! Your life for the boy." The last words as the madman scurried away pounded against Reed's skull. Why the paralysis in that moment? He had been helpless to fight for Jack or to give chase.

He had one option – go to the field where Madge could see his final victory.

The murky beginning of another London township day squeezed into the room. Reed slid upright against the wall and opened his eyes. There was no end to the nightmare. For a moment he was not sure that his legs would work. The cramping spasms caused him to stagger as he began circling the room. At first, he braced himself against the wall. He practiced walking until it seemed natural again. Then he felt life moving upward in him.

He stopped after several cycles when an announcement hung in the air,

"This doesn't need to happen. This is a madman's plan!"

The words hung in the room as if they came from another's mouth. Like a man uncertain of his location, Reed spun on his heels stepped this way and that until he stopped again.

"I will not let my life end this way. It's worth the risk . . . my life and Jack's."

Reed hurried into the room where his belongings had been stashed his first day in the house. Cartons and bags were stacked in disarray where, in his hopelessness, he had dropped those months ago. In the corner he found the Mossberg 20 gauge wrapped in an old blanket. His first recollection of its existence had been only yesterday when he lost Jack. Then he thought of how he might use it to make the trade that Madge demanded.

He searched recklessly through the rest of the cartons until he found the ammunition. The box was old – maybe twenty years. Reed was not a hunter. When his father gave him the shotgun on his twelfth birthday there was great excitement. Since, however, the gun had not been fired more than a dozen times. The shells were almost antique. Reed removed one shell and bounced it in his hand, staring at it. He removed another and the two went in his shirt pocket.

Quickly, he stood. It was an amazing transformation. The heaviness of Reed's walk, the reticent amble, the persona of a man hesitant, all of it disappeared. He swept the shotgun into his hands as he moved swiftly to the kitchen and the exit. It was 7AM. He had five hours to prepare the final act for the madman.

Four hours later he pulled into the parking lot of the Riverside School. Across the way he saw Caren's car. He sat silently behind the wheel of the truck and stared straight ahead. His decision to come here was made an hour earlier as he left the fifth slaughterhouse that morning. He waited.

A smile appeared on Reed's face. He was thinking how close he had come this time. Happiness for him was like a mostly cloudy day. In the open fields around there are those tiny breaks in the overcast. They let sharp laser like shots of sunshine through but the clouds quickly squeezed the sky back to solid gray. The last few months had been a flash of happiness to Reed. In spite of the horror of events around him, Reed came alive.

He groaned aloud. It was likely finished. The crack in the dimness was past. He shook his head in surrender to the familiar. He looked at the clock on the dash. It was thirty minutes from the appointment in the field.

High noon was thirty minutes away.

Reed reviewed the risky strategy. It would take him about 20 minutes to get to the back gate of the field where Madge would be observing. That would give him ten minutes to prepare the scene. Next to him, wrapped in that white heavy paper that butchers use, was the severed hog's head and two plastic bags of blood. Reed calculated the distance necessary between his truck and the wooded area next to the field. He knew that Madge would watch from there. Reed struggled to imagine the view from 60 feet, 100 feet, a hundred yards, and farther. He would drive to the point where Madge could see and hear; more clearly hear than see.

Madge was restrained. He was about to finish his work and finish it well. The Great Spirit had beneficently ordered the circumstances for Madge's convenience. Never would he have thought that the son of one of the invaders would fall into his hands. And now, the brilliance of the final sacrifice – no combat, no frenetic feints and dodges, only a simple and quiet death. Madge, the high priest, the shaman, would watch. From the woods he would sing the song of springtime – the life of his people, The Fire People, would be renewed with the demise of such an old enemy. He carried the enemy's son like a sack of wheat over his shoulder as he marched through to the edge the woods nearest the French Claim. The effect of the tea that Madge had forced the boy to drink had not worn off. Stuffed in Madge's belt was the sparkling pruning knife – just in case the boy's life was required.

The plan is so simple. The son of the Shillinger clan who usurped the land of the people when the white government sent them west would sacrifice himself. The wendigo's mission would be completed with the result that the one possessed, whose life was filled only with the mission of the wendigo, would begin to live again – with a son. If, however, the Shillinger descendent was foolish enough to defy the will of wendigo the final sacrifice would take place and the last Shillinger male would shed his blood on the land of the Fire People. Madge would see to it.

Madge came to the edge of the woods at the base of the familiar hickory. It was a very old tree. Madge remembered times when he came here as a child. The tree and Madge had grown together. A large limb, ten feet above the ground, grew straight and laterally from the trunk. Madge laid the boy on the ground at the base of the tree and climbed to an overhead vantage point. He could see the whole field from there.

He waited.

Reed had decided that Caren needed to know exactly what was about to happen. He sat in the truck and wrote a letter, stuffed it in an envelope and, driving to the entrance of the school, ran in and handed it to the office secretary.

"This is an emergency message for Caren Mack. Please take it to her now."

After speeding through the countryside, Reed was nearing the tiny opening in the fencerow where he would turn when a shadow suddenly slashed across his windshield. As the pick-up swerved into the turn, Reed saw the bird again. It swooped until it nearly touched the earth, then the owl like bird rose slightly and landed on an ancient fence post alongside the cut into the field. Almost immediately the bird resumed flight and Reed stopped to watch. Across the way, a hundred yards from him, the woods began. The bird slowed and began to glide toward the pinnacle of the tallest tree. Reed shook his head like a drunk testing his perception. The strange presence of that huge bird! Especially now!

Most of the feeling in Reed's body was around his eyes. Nevertheless, he held the pick-up steady, steering toward the center of the field. He needed to concentrate. Everything that Madge commanded he would do – up to the end. There were no instructions as to the position of the pick-up in the field – only that it must be in the center. Reed cranked the wheel so that the pick-up was moving in a tight circle. When the woods appeared in the side-view mirror he stopped.

He found the place in the field. He stopped the truck and killed the engine. Silence! He deliberately did not turn toward the woods. But he began scanning the area around the field. When the woods came into view, he studied the detail of the bushy fencerow stretching along the edge. He recognized the tree the bird chose. As he stopped momentarily he thought he saw a dark blob against the trunk just above the ground. A shiver went through him.

"So you came to see. Good for you, you madman! Here's the show. Pay attention!" Reed whispered.

The air was still cold. The longer he sat there carefully calculating each step, the more the windows of the truck misted over.

"That'll help." thought Reed.

Immediately he began to exhale large breaths on the window toward the woods.

"Don't want you to see too well." Reed's one-way conversation continued.

He reached for the butcher's package. He was careful to keep his upper body steady. The observer would not notice that he was preparing a little charade. When the package was unwrapped, Reed crushed the paper and stuffed it into the crack in the passenger seat. The truck filled with the smell of fresh, raw meat. In his hands he held a pig's head. It was comically heavy. Reed tried not to laugh at the irony. "Imagine needing to carry this thing around all your life.' he chuckled.

With the bloody head sitting in his lap staring at his belt buckle, Reed began exaggerating his movement as he stuffed the plastic bag of pig's blood into the mouth of the pig's head. Then he reached for the Mossberg. He held it high in the cab as he moved it in front of his body. He took off his jacket and placed it near him on the seat. Then he loaded a shell into the Mossberg.

From the hickory Madge watched. His eyes followed the truck into the field. Excitement took hold of him. Ten lifetimes ago his ancestors walked the ground in front of him. Blurry images followed the truck into the center of the field. The Fire People had come to see. If all went as Madge had instructed, they would soon break into a ghostly dance. The truck stopped. Madge was patient. The man's slow movements were invisible from the distance. But Madge could wait. He loved the wait. As long as the man was out there, Madge anticipated victory. Several minutes passed.

Suddenly the window on the driver's side exploded outward followed by a pink mist. Then he heard the explosion!

Reed knew that he had to make this work. There was no room for shoddy execution. The view that would draw Madge from the woods to inspect the final carnage would have to be convincing. He could see the dark figure, a simple spot in his vision, high on the tree limb at the edge of the woods. Reed slowly slouched in the corner of the car on the passenger side. Earlier he had adjusted the driver's side view mirror to watch the woods. As he slid downward his hand brought the pig's head upward. As he moved the head up, Reed forced his head to one side resting on his left shoulder. With his other hand he brought the Mossberg into position to the right of his head. At the exact moment that the open barrel met the drooping lips of the gruesome head, the gun exploded blowing the meat into a million pink fragments, splattering the inside of the truck and blasting the window outward.

Reed was motionless. He was also stone deaf. The gun blast happened inches from his right ear. He stared across the cab at the mirror. The wait was endless. Eventually, Reed saw something move. A spot began to descend from one of the trees. Very deliberately Reed reached to the floor to get the container of blood. Without moving his upper body or shoulders opened the second bag of blood and began to splash the pig's blood across the cab. With considerable effort he finally was able to cover the rear window and parts of the windshield with a reddish gore.

"I want you to watch and believe. But I don't want you to see!" muttered Reed.

Chapter Twenty Five

Madge jerked with the explosion. His eyes locked into a stare at the scene in the field. He heard the boy at the base of the tree move in the dry leaves. The sound of feathered wings against the air rushed past Madge's head. It all ended in silence.

The boy was his. His ancestors two generations earlier had found a new place and a new life after the march west, and only a straggling few went east. He would follow the eastern migration and return to Canada, the home of his mother. He looked down at the boy struggling against his bonds and the tape across his mouth. He would set him free as he promised, but he would not send him back. This boy was an orphan. Madge would rescue him from a life without a father.

First, he needed to dance and see the proof that his work here was completed.

He swung from the limb to the trunk and with one movement was on the ground. As he stepped near the bound boy, he playfully rubbed the boy's head. Whirling in a graceful pirouette, he entered the field. He skipped and zigzagged toward the truck, his head thrown back and his arms outspread. Within a few feet of the pick up Madge stopped, and an attitude of reverence transformed his physique. He stepped in slow motion and began to sing.

He circled behind the truck. On the ground around the far side of the vehicle gory pieces of flesh could be seen scattered as far away as twenty feet. Madge walked to the window which was nothing but a ragged fringe of glass particles clinging to the rubber seals around the opening. He turned his body to peer into the cab. At that very moment Madge reached for the knife in the belt. It was too late.

Another roar broke the silence. Standing at the rear of the pick-up, Mossberg waist high, was Reed. Madge never had a chance. The blast hit him square in the face. He fell forward, his hands against the cab. Sliding downward, through the red film that was drifting into his vision Madge looked up. He saw the sun break through the overcast – then nothing.

High in the hickory at the edge of the woods, the huge bird unlocked his head and stretched his wings. He looked down at the boy below – but it was only a glance. There was nothing of interest to see. Pushing off, the animal flew through the trees of the woods, gaining speed until his wondrous ability to soar without crashing into trees made it appear that a straight path had been cut through the woods. Deep in the center of the place the bird rose in a curving loop, came over and under in a 360 degree somersault, and entered a hole in a big rotting maple. The sun was fully uncovered. Soon the air was warm and the owl's eyes closed.

CHAPTER TWENTY SIX

The field was deserted. Near the woods the lone figure of Reed Shillinger strode resolutely in the direction of his son who was now wide-awake and weeping. Kneeling next to the boy, Reed strained at the knots and freed the boy.

"Jack, you're safe. I am safe. Its over." Reed spoke softly as he held the boy to his chest.

In the distance, there was the sound of a car approaching the entrance to the field. Reed glanced in that direction and made certain that it was Caren.

"Dad, are we going to be alright? Is that man going to follow us?" Jack asked.

"No, he's not going to bother anyone – Ever! Let's get out of here."

They walked toward Caren who had left her car and broke into a run. Reed was still trembling uncontrollably when she stepped into his arms. Their embrace caught Jack between them, but never before had he felt this protected. The sun was shining in a clear sky about halfway between the horizons and a little to the south. Caren's face was buried in Reed's shoulder, and Reed's face was turned to the sky. When both opened their drenched eyes they squinted. The brightness was enough to cover the fear – to squeeze it out.

Still holding each other, the three walked away.

About The Author

Merlyn Seitz was born in Monroe, Michigan in 1942. Until he left Michigan to attend Capital University in Columbus, Ohio he lived with his family on two farms in London Township and in Exeter Township, Monroe County, Michigan.

Beginning in his college years, he has written stories that bring to life the many fantasies and imaginings of his more reflective moments. Many of the images and events in the novel, Overcast, became a part of his mental library many years ago. The story of Reed Shillinger and Madge has been waiting patiently to be written for years. One of his strongest memories of the wonderful world of southeast Michigan is the lack of blue skies. Weather statistics show that approximately two thirds of the time the sky is cloudy. He has always believed that a person's place of origin and history can provide the stuff of self-redemption. Nevertheless,

Merlyn Seitz is proud of the history and heritage of Monroe County. The people who live there and have died there are a part of him.

He is married and the father of a daughter and a son. His ancestors settled in the Monroe area in the mid 1800's. He lives on a farm in central Ohio where he continues to serve as a pastor and dabbles in activities first learned in Exeter and London townships.

Working as a Lutheran pastor, he has lived in Ethiopia and several cities and towns in Ohio. In 1996 he received a doctor's degree in the area of research into the place and significance of narrative for human self-understanding. In 2004 he co-edited "Mission To Ethiopia: An American Lutheran Memoir 1957-2003" published by Kirkhouse Publishing.

Printed in the United States
63321LVS00001B/55-63